D0571887

NINE▲MAN▲TREE

by Robert Newton Peck

Random House  New York

▲ ▲ ▲

Nine Man Tree is dedicated to a friend and hunting buddy,
Mr. Harry Oshman. His advice helped write this book. He is
a fun guy, a polite Florida gentleman, and an able woodsman.
A straight shooter. Above all, his respect for nature and
wildlife merit my respect for him.

—Robert Newton Peck
Longwood, Florida

Copyright © 1998 by Robert Newton Peck
Cover art copyright © 1998 by Richard Waldrep

All rights reserved under International and Pan-American Copyright
Conventions. Published in the United States by Random House, Inc.,
New York, and simultaneously in Canada by Random House of Canada
Limited, Toronto. Distributed by Random House, Inc., New York.

www.randomhouse.com/kids/

Library of Congress Cataloging-in-Publication Data
Peck, Robert Newton
Nine man tree by Robert Newton Peck.
p. cm.
Summary: In Depression-era Florida, young Yoolee attempts to assume
the responsibility of protecting his family from an unspeakable horror
stalking the swamplands.
ISBN 0-679-89257-5
[1. Family life—Florida—Everglades—Fiction.
2. Everglades (Fla.)—Fiction. 3. Wild boar—Fiction.] I. Title.
PZ7.P339Ni   1998 [Fic]—dc21 97-43624

Printed in the United States of America
10 9 8 7 6 5 4 3 2

Robert Newton Peck on the left, wearing cowboy hat.
Harry Oshman on the right.
And a 480-pound wild boarhog.

▲ Prologue ▲

FLORIDA
1931

▲ ▲ ▲
_____

The swamp water lay still and black.

Beneath his bare, muddy feet the barge's hull hissed across a floating bed of weeds, slowed to silence, then nosed ahead by another push of the pole. For countless years Henry Old Panther had carved each of his many dugouts from a fallen log. Lately, as his legs were neither young nor sturdy, and also because of a crippled foot, the flat barge felt steadier than a canoe.

The Calusa could not remember his age, knowing only that the charcoal of his hair had gradually burned away to ashes. How long had his hair been white? For a number of fingers and toes. Henry's children had grandchildren. His family had moved up north to Ochopee and wore the white man's clothes. The last time he had brought a gift, a dead rabbit, they hadn't known how to skin or gut it. The rabbit had been dishonored: thrown away and not eaten. After that, Henry forgot all of their faces.

No matter.

Soon the Spirit Mother would beckon him, perhaps as a bird's song, to leave life behind and seek the Nine Man Tree, a cypress taller than the others, so massive as to require nine men, all holding hands in a circle, to reach around the base of its gray, majestic trunk.

When a Calusa warrior was chosen to ascend the Nine Man Tree, reaching the topmost branches of green lace, he continued upward, never returning, because he had been called to climb beyond the clouds.

Henry was not ready to die.

Not quite.

It would not be gallant to accept death when he still might sing or dance around the fire of life. So, every day, regardless of how long it took to coax the painful stiffness from the crooked knuckles of his hands, Henry Old Panther forced himself to board the raft and to perform his assumed mission.

Ahead, an egret landed on a half-submerged log, folded her wings, then lifted a leg and balanced upon the other, a single stem of a white-feathered lily.

"I will not disturb you, my bird friend," Henry silently told the egret, "for it was perhaps your grandmother's grandmother who taught me how to wait with serenity."

Squinting in the misty gray evening, he rested his pole, now content merely to drift, observe. The egret stood motionless until a frog made a fatal move. Poking his head above the dark surface, close to a cypress knee, the bullfrog created a ripple.

As its ring enlarged, Henry noticed.

So did the white egret.

It took three long breaths of time for the bird's free leg to unflex, extend, and finally touch the water one step closer to the frog. The rear leg, in no greater haste, did likewise. Then five unhurried steps, as though the feathered one knew no hunger. Without warning, her curved neck abruptly straightened into a long white lance; a yellow rapier of a beak spiked into the bullfrog, hoisting him high. Struggling, legs kicking silvery beads of water, he almost instantly disappeared to become a squirming bulge in her gullet.

Henry Old Panther nodded an approving tribute to the egret's wisdom. All able hunters merit admiration.

As the egret's legs jacked, then stiffened, and wide wings lofted her off to another hammock, the Calusa poled away, also to hunt. Not to fill his own body. This evening, as on many others, he pursued prey for another's belly, to kill in order to preserve life.

The sun had already set.

Almost all of the colorful fruit-and-flower clouds had drained away, slowly softened by dusk. As he rafted across the black Florida water, Henry knew that it was time for possums to emerge from the leather ferns that grew up taller than a man's head. Night goaded them with an eagerness to eat, and a hungry animal could often be careless. Once Henry Old Panther too had been unwary. Years ago, before his lower leg had been gnawed and crushed by the ugly one, he had stalked his game on foot.

Now he needed a barge.

With every push the Calusa skimmed almost silently, never lifting his pole from the water, listening to a quilt of lily pads whispering their soft green secrets to the mossy bottom of his craft.

Time had whitened Henry's eyes as well as his hair. But as his eyesight failed, his ears told him many stories, the murmurings of a swamp, an orchestra of sounds. Each individual noise or note made him wiser.

A familiar crunching noise froze him motionless.

He heard teeth, the sharp, pointed fangs of a possum snapping the small bones of a fish.

Gently, and with patience, as the egret had taught him so many years ago, the Calusa's fingers released the pole. It now floated quietly behind, tied to the raft by a vine lanyard. A hand that had held the long pole now gripped a shorter one.

A hunting weapon.

Arm raised, cocking the spear over his right shoulder, Henry Old Panther waited for the sound to approach along the hammock's mud bank. If the noise moved away, so let it, for another would approach.

Where there was a single possum, there were many.

As the possum moved closer, Henry inhaled her scent. A female in heat.

The chewing noises grew louder and varied. Teeth were now cracking the brittle shells of freshwater mussels, about two barge lengths away, he guessed. Squinting, he could see the possum's white tail, a hairless whip lashing as she fed. Against his palm the spear's shaft felt eager, yet Henry restrained it with a subtle squeeze of fingers. Not yet. Not quite yet. Barely breathing, he made himself into a tree. No motion. Hardly a heartbeat. For an instant the possum looked up, her black eyes shining at him. Satisfied that he was merely part of the vegetation, she lowered her whiskered snout once again to feed.

Now.

Through his teeth Henry made a possum's hiss, a call that brought her erect, paws up. Striking as a serpent, the lance punctured the possum, passing neatly through the body and shattering the spine. The kill was swift and clean. A dead possum was retrieved to twitch on the damp, mossy deck of the barge.

An aroma of fresh meat taunted Henry's nose, aching his innards for a fire and a feast. But no. The kill would serve a higher purpose. Perhaps it would save the lives of a pair of young ones, the white children with corn silk hair, a color between silver and gold. The two children, who did not even suspect that he was alive, were so beautiful to behold. Henry Old Panther had always been fascinated by pretty objects that shined in sunlight.

With luck, he might hunt and kill for many more evenings, to allow the corn silk children to stay alive. Their mother and father didn't seem aware of the danger that lurked and stalked nearby.

Henry Old Panther surely knew.

He had heard the chomping of powerful jaws, the snarls, and smelled the rotting remains of a bull, a gator, and several bears. Such a huge beast could slay anything it attacked. Henry understood, because he had tracked the monster who had maimed his leg to this area of the swamp. He'd become too crippled to hunt the critter with a spear, yet he was still alert enough to divert its hunger from those youthful ones who wore corn silk hair so delightful that their heads seemed to sing. Perhaps the pair of children were gifts to him from the Spirit Mother, the last pretty things his weakened eyes would ever admire.

Tonight's possum would feed the evil one, so its tusks might not rip apart the gold and silver children. Henry Old Panther had even named the giant beast he fed but feared to attack.

Hell Hog.

▲ Chapter 1 ▲

"Yoolee?"

As he heard his name being hollered, Yoolee Tharp lay on his belly in a patch of late-afternoon sunshine, watching a horse-head grasshopper gnaw the edge of a heart-shaped moonvine leaf. It made a faint munching noise and looked to measure nearly four inches. Closing his eyes, Yoolee imagined that he was tiny enough to ride that hopper as a pony.

"Yoolee! Where you at?" It was his daddy's snarl. "Answer up, boy, or I'll be coming with my deer-hide belt to locate you and whup ya proper."

"Ain't ya cut enough welts on that child?" Yoolee heard his mother say. Her voice was some softer. Yet there was also a hardness inside Ruth Ann's words, a sawtooth sound that had been notched into her by living under a roof with Velmer Tharp.

He was growling at her. "Shut yer mouth, woman. You want another cuff across yer face?"

"Soon," Yoolee whispered, stroking the grasshopper very lightly with a fingertip, "I'll be plenty growed to fetch Mama and Havilah away from this bad place."

He didn't know exactly where they might go. It would be somewhere a spate off from Velmer's ornery temper. The three of them could make a happy home where flowers would grow beneath mockingbird music. And nobody'd be cussing or smelling of jug juice. Many times his back had smarted from the metal end of the belt. When old Velmer gripped it by the buckle, Yoolee could abide the lashing of leather. But the pain of getting buckled was tough to swallow. And it drew blood.

Although he was hungry, Yoolee refused to return to the shack, not caring if he missed out on supper. Havilah might sneak a few biscuits to him. His sister was only eight, three years younger, yet often treated him as though he were a doll instead of a big brother. Plenty of times she'd washed his bruises with salt water and then bandaged him with layers of lotus leaves to fend off any insects.

At night, if she reasoned he was still hurting, Havilah would sing him to sleep, making up words to her own little songs, tiny high-up notes that trilled like a lark.

Velmer never beat on Havilah.

With her he did a lot sorrier. Whenever she'd wander down to the crick, skin off her little sack dress, and wash herself, he'd hide among the low-growing palmetto to spy on his daughter. Yoolee had caught him doing it. That was the main reason the two of them hated each other so dreadful. After that, Velmer turned his belt around so the buckle would cut worse than sickness.

"I never told Mama," he said to the grasshopper. "Because it'd maybe put damage on her deeper than a belt could do."

Nor had he reported any of this to Havilah. Instead he'd merely advised his sister to do her private crick bathing at times when Velmer'd gone off with the scattergun to plume-hunt birds. She'd asked how come. So he told her a little white story that he'd made up about good manners and being polite enough to perform certain things alone. Like taking a leak. Or washing up.

"You mustn't trust everybody, Havilah," he had warned her.

For some reason that made her smile until all the freckles danced across her face. She said, "I trust *you*."

The sunset dimmed. Far to the southwest, beyond the Ten Thousand Islands and over the great gulf, dry drums of thunder rolled closer with every muffled boom, followed by a misty rain that drenched a day to a gray wet wool of night. Jagged rivers of white-hot lightning carved the purple sky into a massive block of marble large enough to be God's headstone. With each crash the vines on the gumbo-limbo tree trembled as though afraid. Back at the shack people again might be calling his name to come in from the storm. Yet a war of noise prevented his hearing their voices.

As the storm crawled away, inching eastward over the Everglades, the rain also retreated. All that remained were the countless taps of raindrops.

Nonetheless Yoolee waited.

It made little sense to return to Velmer's rasping rage. To eat supper, Yoolee would have to absorb the man's abuse, and a meal of grits and collards wasn't worth it. No hunger pang cut sharp enough to prod him homeward. Thus he stayed among the damp aromas of wild orange, muscadine, and lancewood until the night darkened and deepened, dried by delicate breezes.

Rain had driven much of the animal life to shelter, yet as the storm disappeared, all nocturnal forms appeared to hunt and be hunted. An owl hooted. In response, a three-quarter moon emerged, inviting Yoolee Tharp to stand in its light and brush the moisture and mud from his only garment, a bib overall once dark blue but now faded to softness in both color and texture.

"Yoolee," his sister had recently warned, "you best prosper your duds. Because when you outgrows 'em, they might be mine."

When his bare foot stepped to snap a fallen gumbo twig, the timid sound caused him to freeze. A chilly feeling, as though unknown eyes were searching him, whispered a caution to stay still. Yoolee inhaled the scents as though they were spices, most of them familiar—except one, a wisp that willed him to wonder: What? Or who? It wasn't anything green. Nothing rooted in the deep layers of peaty muck that oozed up between his toes.

His nostrils detected a smell that walked, breathed, and hunted.

While he peered through the pond apples hanging from spindle limbs that drooped with their weight, the foreign odor again flinched his nose. It seemed alarmingly alive, mean and menacing. Not human, because the stink was too strong.

"What are you?" he asked the darkness.

Sneaking a few steps nearer to the distant shack, Yoolee could hear his daddy's grating voice. A hard object was hurled at somebody, then all seemed to simmer and still. When old Velmer was shirttail drunk, his legs couldn't quit wobbling, and he'd sort of fall down wherever he stood. Once he passed out, there was no rousing him, not even if their shack was burning.

Yoolee waited in the night.

Both of his parents were asleep when he final crept indoors and up the short wall ladder to the cramped loft to join Havilah on the tattered tick they shared.

"Where you been?" Her eyes popped open.

His hand quickly covered her mouth. "Outside.

Please don't wake up the folks, on account I'm too tuckered to scoot off again."

Havilah eased her brother's hand off her face.

"You hungry, Yool?" When he nodded, her fingers slid beneath the muslin pillow to pull out four biscuits, a sweet potato in its skin, plus an ear of roasted corn.

"Thanks, Hav."

With a biscuit in his mouth, Yoolee ripped the warm corn shucks off, one by one, being careful not to make any noise. As he chewed, Havilah stretched a hand up to the top rafter and produced a tin cup. "I also sneaked you some goat's milk. Because corn usual turns you thirsty."

"You're a star of a sister."

Knees clasped under her resting chin, Havilah watched him chomp the corn ear. "You know, Yoolee, you make more racket eating than most people do when they talk."

"That's because I'm so blessed empty. I could about eat a gator raw. My gut couldn't have lasted another breath without chow."

In the dark, Yoolee could feel his sister's wide eyes studying him. "Yool, what's it like to be eleven?"

"Bigger'n ten. And a whole doggone mile longer than eight. Soon I'll be coming up twelve. Then thirteen, and that's *manhood,* like Mama heard be ancient Hebrew."

She wiped corn off his chin. "You still are paltry little to stand up a man. Men shave. And they ramble off to work."

"Who told you?"

"Mama."

After swallowing the last biscuit without much bothering to chew, he whispered, "Hav, you're a good ol' sister, but you don't know beans about getting growed up, like me."

She poked him. "I know a thing you don't. Mama told me during her stand at the cookstove getting supper. It's sort of a secret. Soon we're to git some company."

He felt excited. "Who's coming?"

"It's somebody nice who ain't visited for a spell. When she told me, Mama almost smiled. Now I bet you be itching to know real bad."

Yoolee's head fell to the other pillow, formerly a flour sack. "Not me. I'm too tired to worry it, even if the person who's coming here is President Hoover. So you can keep your secret until sunup."

Closing his eyes and letting out a heavy sigh, he pretended to be falling asleep. He knew full well that Hav wouldn't be able to nestle the news to herself. In less than a count of three, she'd bust it out wide open. One...two...

"Promise if I tell you, you won't let on to Daddy. He ain't to know, Mama says, because Pa can't abide who's coming. Hates his guts." Havilah paused for a breather. "Give up?"

"Okay, I give up, Hav. Who's coming?"

"Uncle Bib."

▲ Chapter 2 ▲

On the following morning Uncle Bib didn't show up, but someone else came to the Tharps' hammock in a kicker boat.

Before somebody cut the engine, both Yoolee and Havilah went racing through the wet ferns, not expecting to see Uncle Bib, who usual arrived in a Ford. Yet their visitor wasn't a stranger. He was the deputy sheriff, Joonyer Cobb.

After he had moored the motorboat to a mangrove elbow, Joonyer pulled on a pair of rubber boots and waded to shore through the green scum of frog spit. He looked handsome in his suntan constable's uniform, an ammunition belt with a row of cartridges, and a pistol that was asleep in its leather holster. On its butt, a braided lanyard looped to his belt. He was a shiny sight to see.

"Hey," Joonyer said, his mouth cracking a slight smile, "tell me, how's it by y'all?"

"Good," Yoolee said. He felt happy on any day that Velmer wasn't around. Besides, he'd always liked Joonyer well enough.

"Fine, thank you," Havilah answered politely, making Yoolee feel as though she were correcting him. At times that little gal could be a backside boil.

Joonyer Cobb, according to what Yoolee had usual heard, wasn't exactly a young man. Instead, he was nearing fifty, with more than a spatter of gray hair. But his pa, the one everybody referred to as Senior, was still the main sheriff, although he was seventy years and then some. People kept voting Senior into the constable's office, because nobody ever ran against him. Senior Cobb, according to public opinion—which was favorable—had a way of living and let live. He kept the peace and ignored anybody who engaged in the pastime of moonlight farming, which was distilling whiskey.

"Good ol' Senior," many a citizen commented, "looks his best whenever he's looking the other way."

Everyone agreed that Joonyer was a cooperative chip off a comfortable block. For certain he would get elected for sheriffing someday. Not necessarily soon.

"Your folks to home?" Joonyer asked.

Yoolee hesitated before answering. He'd long ago noticed that whenever the *law* showed up, at the first faint sound of a kicker boat, Velmer Tharp drifted into the scrub, like morning mist.

"Mama's here," he told Joonyer. The constable's smile brightened. "But I don't guess you're fixing to arrest *her,* are ya?" Yoolee already knew the answer to that question, on account that Joonyer Cobb came often to the shack for social visits. This pleased Yoolee. His mother acted near to happy with Joonyer abiding.

The peace officer shook his head. "Not hardly. However, we all just maybe got ourselfs a problem. I'm not coon-dogging anyone. Just trying to share a scrap of information. Or swap."

"What's the matter?" Yoolee asked.

"Tell," Hav insisted. "Please tell."

"Well now, what say the three of us amble up to high ground, to your place, so's I can relate it once instead of twice. You both agreeable?"

"Makes sense to me," Yoolee told Joonyer. "But I ain't sure that my sister can wait to hear anything. Or to repeat it."

Havilah poked him.

"Your hounds tied?" Joonyer asked with a wink. "I can't fancy approaching somebody's residence if their dogs are loose. They don't seem to be barking."

"Both be tied up," Hav said.

"Tied or untied," Yoolee added, "them two dogs of ours are too blessed lazy to do much except yawn in the morning and then after they'd be rested up from that, scratch away the evening."

As the three of them walked through the pines, Yoolee wanted to tell Joonyer that what the Tharps needed the most police protection from was vicious old Velmer. But he held quiet on that matter. His mind, however, was pondering on what sort of protecting their family would need, as they lived closed to lonesome.

Ruth Ann appeared at the doorway of the shack, drying her hands on a rag and squinting from the early sun that sifted down through the cypress lace. Seeing Joonyer, she quickly smoothed her hair.

"Howdo, Miz Tharp," Joonyer called, pulling off his cowboy hat and waving it at her.

"Morning, Joon. And I told you plenty times, there's no need to call me Miz Tharp. I ain't uppity. Besides," she smiled at the deputy, "I'm younger than you are. You knowed me back when I was Ruth Ann Alderkirk, which I wish I still was."

"Yes'm," Joonyer mumbled. "Me too." He flushed a bit, as though not quite knowing what next to say, and looked down at his muddy boots.

"What brings ya?" Yoolee's mother asked. "If you're here to fetch Velmer, well, he's off somewheres. Gun's gone, so you might reckon he's plume-hunting. If he keeps up, won't be a parakeet or finch left to blow apart. Makes ya wonder how people up north do with all them feathers."

"'Deed so." Joonyer eased his hat back on. "Today, guess I'm sort of here official." He smiled at Ruth Ann. "Reason I come is there's been trouble nearby." He pointed over his shoulder. "Less'n a mile down-crick.

Seems like one of the Baggitt youngsters, eldest one, a boy named Walton, up and disappeared. A sorry shame."

Ruth Ann made a face as though she wasn't really hearing news. "Oh, that boy's run away plenty. Slinks home whenever he's hungry."

Joonyer nodded. "S'pect so. But this time's some different. His people found one of Walton's boots, his hat, and part of a tore-up shirt. No sign of Walton. The shirt, what little got left of it, certain was bloody."

Ruth Ann raised her eyebrows. "Calusas?"

Joonyer Cobb shook his head. "Not likely. Far as I know, the Nation's been peaceable as Sunday church. Nary a peep from their direction. In fact, last evening, right after I'd took on home from the Baggitt place, I got on the contraption and cranked up Sheriff Durance in Jerome. He reported it's all quiet up yonder." Joonyer rested a big boot on the edge of the stoop. "Besides, far as either Senior or I can witness, the Calusa are neighborly decent and never been cannibal."

"What's a cannibal?" Hav wanted to know.

"People that eat other people," Joonyer blurted out, then looked as if he regretted it. To ease himself, he returned to the matter of Walton Baggitt. "Anyhows, one of the younger kids found something and brung it home."

"What was it?" Ruth Ann asked.

"A hand. Part of one."

"No." Her mouth stayed open.

"For certain, it was Walton's, on account he'd fashioned hisself a ring. A bent-around nail, with a tiny little *W* scratched into the metal. Still on his finger, even though the hand was in poorly condition. Chewed, and bled to a deadly white. Looked to me like the hand of a ghost." Joonyer shrugged. "Believe me, Ruth Ann, the sight startled me more'n a bother. A pitiful thing to see. Like the ring was alive and shiny, but that healthy boy be dead. And died horrible."

"That was his ring, all right," Yoolee piped up. "I seen it to his finger plenty of times. A horseshoe-nail ring."

"You after Velmer?" Ruth Ann asked the deputy in a dry voice.

"No. No way. All I aim to do here is warn you to corral the young 'uns close to home. If you hear a strange sound or smell an unusual whiff of something, stay to the indoors. And you might tell Velmer to keep his shotgun loaded, but not with bird dust or buckshot. Advise him to use a ball, a slug. Because if this is what I suspect..."

Joonyer's voice faded off, as though he lacked the gumption to finish up whatever had gotten stuck on his tongue. Perhaps to rest his mind about Walton, he pulled a Red Man pouch from his back pocket, unrolled it, and dipped a pinch of tobacco into his cheek.

Yoolee saw his ma frown.

"Why," asked Ruth Ann, "do you have to chew that cud?"

Shifting the wad, Joonyer answered, "Well, I reckon I need a hobby, seeing as I never won me a wife."

"And you blessed won't ever wed one," Ruth Ann warned him, "with a mass of manure in your mouth."

To Yoolee's dismay, Joonyer Cobb turned away and spat out his Red Man. Then, wiping his chin, he changed the subject. "By the way, Ruth Ann, what's the gauge of Velmer's gun? As I recall, used to be a twelve."

"Ain't. It's a twenty," Yoolee said. "We also got a four-ten, which is a right good all-arounder."

"Like fun. A four-ten," said Joonyer, "is a peashooter. And just maybe, against what's down-crick, even a twenty-gauge wouldn't do squat or make it flinch. Because of the storm, there weren't no paw prints in the mud to determine if we're dealing with a panther or a bear."

"Maybe a gator?" Ruth Ann asked.

"I doubt. On account that no bull gator or croc would be wandering that far from water. The remains, what little of, was located on high ground. Senior and me both suspect different. If this dreadful thing's what we imagine, we all got one horror of a worry. A critter such as this meat-eater has most likely growed a hide close to iron. Twenty-gauge, even with a single-ball load, would hardly tickle its ribs."

Ruth Ann moved to stand between her children. She rested a hand on Yoolee's shoulder. The other pulled Havilah closer. "If you come to fright us, Joonyer," she said, "you're doing it. Can't guess when my man'll come home. Sometimes he strays for half a week. What'll I do?"

"Herd the whelps inside. Bolt the door. As usual, I'll be back regular to check on y'all. Meanwhile, keep vigilant. Big animals got a big smell. I'll be listening for Velmer's gun, and when I trace him down, I will pronto him home."

"Thank you, Joon."

"Just doing my job." The constable paused. "You know, in y'all's case, it might be more'n that. I'd feel poorly if anything bad happened to you or your brood."

Ruth Ann nodded. "I know." Her voice softened and her eyes were smiling.

No more was said. Yet it was certain enough to make Yoolee understand that maybe some words wanted to be spoke. Joonyer Cobb, he had noticed over the years, always seemed to have a handy excuse for coming to visit the Tharps, and it wasn't just to check on old Velmer.

As the large deputy left, heading down-ground for his kicker boat, Yoolee Tharp reached behind his mother's back to touch Havilah.

Her trembling hand met his.

▲ Chapter 3 ▲

Yoolee was watching his sister.

Girls, he thought, were aplenty different from boys. He was still a kid, but Havilah, even at age eight, was already a small woman.

"How do we cook this, Mama?" she asked. "I reckoned we'd boil it all in a pot of water."

"S'pose we can. But I usual roll the okra in cornmeal and then it's ready for the frypan. Yoolee," Ruth Ann said, turning to look at him, "we're precious low on stove wood. While it's still light outside, go hustle up some dry." As he started to unbolt the door, she added, "Best you stay close to the house. If'n that thing, whatever be, is rustling around out yonder, never mind the kindling. Yoolee, you just hustle for home."

"I'll do such."

"Don't meander up into the pines. Ground up there's lots firmer than right here. Cypress be good as pine wood. The stove'll make do even with hook-thorn palmetto, long as it's seasoned brown enough to burn." While he was slipping out the door, she offered

27

a final warning. "Once ya hear our dogs barking, or the goat bleat, you scamper back."

A minute later, Yoolee was snaking through the ferns that always grew thick in the black muck. Closer to the shallow crick, the saw grass was higher than ferns and sprouted considerable above a grown man. Near the freshet, where he and Havilah always took the bucket for water, he could hear otters splashing at play. An otter certain did savvy enjoyment. Otters deserved respect because they had the courage to flit and flirt among alligators and take pleasure in slipping down a mudslide. Every otter that Yoolee had ever seen seemed to have a face that was laughing at the entire world.

Between two large clumps of saw grass a duck paddled lazily. Squinting, he could see it was a teal with blue wings.

Glancing over his shoulder to make sure of how he could make a quick retreat, Yoolee noticed the stilts that supported their shack. They were longer than he was tall, holding the little house above the ground so that rattlers could crawl under it instead of through it. Underneath, it was damp and dark, and during the summer hot spells, both their dogs slept away the daylight there.

At night, being hounds, Possy and Ladylove prowled and howled, often absent until morning. At sunup they'd turn up muddy, tired, and often dragging a carcass.

"Last night, y'all brung something back," he said to the dogs. "I was awake and heard it all, right before the first light."

Maybe, the boy considered, he'd best break himself of the habit of talking out loud to nobody except little ol' Yoolee Tharp. For years he'd done it, because there wasn't yet a Havilah to play with, and later, as a tyke, she didn't venture outdoors too often. Lately his sister had started to follow after him almost everywhere he went, sneaking up behind him on tiptoe to yell "Boo." Her idea of a joke.

"Hav, don't do it today, on account there's ample for me to fret about without your shadowing."

His mother usual told him to bring mostly an armload of baking wood that could offer up a steady heat and eventual settle to a cool bed. There didn't seem to be dry wood of enough size to haul home. The twigs were either too wet or too skimpy.

Moving farther into the brush brought him close to a black-water pond, too deep for wading in places.

"Ain't fixing to poke around in there."

Just as he said it, Yoolee heard a loud crack of sound, a familiar noise to any Florida swamper's ear. One report, then silence. He knew right off what caused it: the jaws of a gator crunching the shell of a big snapper turtle.

The instant death made Yoolee Tharp shudder. But then with a slight shrug he accepted the turtle's end for what it was: merely an alligator's meal. Recently he had sort of concluded that the Glades were a home for many forms of life—and as many manners of death. To have one meant having the other. It all balanced, like whenever he and Havilah pumped up and down on a seesaw.

"Walton Baggitt."

The name seemed to echo on the gray hanging moss as though it were a ghost. Then, like Walton, it died to stillness, swallowed up and gone forever.

Yoolee felt cold.

A year or so ago, Walton had flicked out his fish knife and whittled something really special for Yoolee. It was a basswood turkey call. A person didn't blow through it like a duck call but picked a thin wooden slat inside a chamber to make it *cluck*. It sounded close to a turkey hen. Yoolee hadn't yet shot a gobbler with the four-ten. So far he had merely fired and missed. Velmer liked to grumble that the boy's efforts at turkey hunting be a sorry waste of shells, and his young'un couldn't hunt worth a bound-up crap.

"How'll he ever be able to shoot straight if'n he don't never pull a trigger?" his mother had scolded Velmer. "Learn him how, that's what you ought, seeing as you're his pa."

"Am I?" Velmer had snorted. "I ain't so sure."

Just then, from the corner of his eye, Yoolee thought he spotted movement. It was only a few leaves on a low branch of custard apple, yet he knew something had caused the twig to budge. Peering closer, he spotted a doe slowly dropping her nose for a dainty sip of spring water. As she drank, a few gentle rings began to swell on the dark surface. The doe lifted her head slightly, the soft brown eyes appearing to look down at a mirror of water, as though to admire her reflection.

Yoolee smiled.

He'd seen his mama and Havilah do likewise in their one little looking glass. That gesture, he figured, was just a thing that female folks do.

Then, in an instant, the doe's nostrils flared and her ears twitched. In less than a blink she darted off through the greenery and out of sight, creating hardly a sound. Something, no doubt, had spooked her.

As he stood there, Yoolee's flesh began to sprout goose bumps. He got a clammy feeling, as though something bad was going to happen any second. Earlier he'd been hungry for okra, but now the desire for food abruptly left him. There was, however, an emptiness that remained in his belly that he couldn't explain away. It was as though his body had been hollowed out, a bit like the inside of Uncle Bib's guitar. And his innards had turned into strings, pulling tighter with every twist of time.

"The first musicians," Uncle Bib had once told Yoolee and Havilah, "were hunters. While waiting for game to come along, they'd fight the boredom by using their thumbs to strum the strings of their hunting bows. Because each bow got strung to a different tightness, the notes were all of varying pitch."

Yoolee took a deep breath.

Then, before he could let it out, an overpowering smell invaded his nose, a stink like nothing else in the swamp. Strong, evil, and mean, a scent that intended to haunt or hurt.

Picking up a few short sticks, Yoolee prepared to make a hurried dash for home. Nearby, whatever it was was snorting in the palmetto thicket as though it didn't care who heard. It had to be a big brute, and plenty powerful. Then Yoolee heard a kind of breathing sound that came in a series of grunts, one that chased him home on a run.

Winded, nearing the shack, he glanced over his shoulder to check if anything was following. No sign, and no more grunting. As he reached the stoop, both Ladylove and Possy stood to greet him, their thin tails wagging. Possy came toward him and Yoolee used a bare foot to stroke her, his arms being loaded with wood. The other hound, however, stayed put just beneath the shade's edge. She balked at leaving a large bone.

A few steps closer to Ladylove, and Yoolee Tharp stopped dead. His mouth fell open and he dropped about half of the firewood.

The bone was from a human leg.

▲ Chapter 4 ▲

"Yool."

As he lay on the sleeping tick, a small finger was poking Yoolee's ribs, disturbing his dream. It was night, hardly the time to be awake, so Yoolee refused to open his eyes.

"Pa's home, Yoolee." He recognized his sister's whisper and received another sharp jab. "And he's brung two people here. They all be talking down below."

"So listen," Yoolee said, still not fully awake.

"I'm trying to," Havilah said. "But I can't make head or tail what's they be yapping about."

He opened an eye. Sure enough, old Velmer'd got home, along with a couple of strange voices. In the loft, from behind the hanging tarp, his mother begged for a little quiet.

"Roll over and play dead, woman," Velmer told her. "I'm trying to rig an important business deal."

Peering down from the other loft where he and Havilah slept, Yoolee first noticed the feeble amber light from a lit candle. Three tin cups sat on the eating table beside a half-gallon glass jug that Yoolee figured wasn't filled with water. An elbow knocked one of the cups off the table, and it clanked onto the floor. After a male voice let out a cuss word, a shadow bent over to retrieve the cup, then banged it a couple of whacks on the table to let the others know it was empty.

It got filled.

Awake now, Yoolee was listening. One voice was Velmer's scratching drawl. The other two sounded unfamiliar, sort of uppity, the way Yoolee imagined city people talked. Sure enough, the strangers had come from Miami. They said so.

"Bryce and I have been on numerous hunting expeditions," one of the men was saying. "We're experienced and well armed."

"What Hampton says is true," the other man said. "We've shot elephant in Africa, so we're not in the least intimidated by any kind of game here in some Florida backwater."

Velmer snorted. "Is that so? Well, according to what Joonyer Cobb's been spreading around…"

"Who," Bryce asked, "is Junior Cobb? A child?"

"Oh, he's Senior's boy, which makes Joonyer a deputy sheriff," Velmer explained in a slurred tone. "Senior is his daddy, but he's seventy past and ain't around too continuous. Just draws his paycheck and lets Joonyer handle most of the legwork."

"What concerns us," Hampton said to Velmer, "is *your* ability and *not* this Junior Cobb's. Before we retain you as a guide, exactly what are your qualifications?"

Velmer scratched himself. "My what?"

"Do you know the whereabouts of this particular animal? We want to learn where he feeds and sleeps as well as the times of day. We need someone to flush him out."

Yoolee saw Velmer pour another drink before answering. "Oh, I've cut down on more'n one of them awesomes. You gents won't locate nobody keener'n me on that score. Ya see, hunting's my job. It's how I work a living."

"Unlike you," said Hampton, "we are not after parakeets."

"My partner's right," Bryce broke in. "If you're capable enough to escort us to the right spot at the ripe moment, and we bag this trophy, we are willing to pay you a handsome reward."

Velmer's cup stopped at his lips. "How much?"

"One hundred dollars."

Old Velmer flinched, then coughed, spilling whiskey all over his shirt and the tabletop. Yoolee had to cover his own mouth and Hav's to keep both of them mum. It took a spell for Velmer to recover before he could sputter out even a word.

"A hunerd bucks?"

Both of the Miami men nodded.

"Providing," Bryce warned, "that our hunt is successful. Included in this fee will be your obtaining all assistance necessary to haul the carcass to our vehicle."

"No bother." Velmer took another stiff gulp of spirit. "You gentlemen can certain bank on me. When Velmer Tharp do business, he always holds up his end of a bargain."

The two men looked at each other.

As they did so, the thought crept into Yoolee's brain that Velmer might be getting taken, but his pa was too greedy to see through the trickery. True, there might be a trophy. Yoolee doubted that there'd be any hundred dollars.

"Do we start out tomorrow?" Bryce asked.

"Shucks, no." Velmer pointed at the door. "If'n we wait, somebody else might come along and shoot at what's rightly our. Best we git going right sudden."

Velmer stood up, but not in a very steady way, because he was gripping the table's edge for support. To Yoolee, his pa didn't seem prepared to go thrashing around in the brush at night in order to scare whatever had tore apart Walton Baggitt. These Miami slicks were playing his dumb old daddy for a sucker.

"Thanks for the whiskey," Velmer said. "Ya can't

beat homemade for sealing a deal." He spat on his right hand. "So let's shake on it."

They all shook.

"Yoolee," Havilah whispered in his ear, "is Pa really going to git paid a whole hundred dollars?"

"He probable won't git even a hundred pennies. Now be still, on account they all be fixing to leave."

"A hundred pennies is a lot of money."

"Sort of. Because you and I only got thirteen hid in our can. Our old man's a fool if he thinks these two ginks'll fork over a hundred bucks."

Velmer thought so. As Yoolee could see in the candlelight, his daddy was smiling with what few teeth he had. Then he turned to take his twenty-gauge from its pegs on the wall.

"You won't need a gun, Mr. Tharp."

Velmer looked confused. "How come?"

"Well," Bryce said, "because Hampton and I, as we informed you earlier, have high-powered rifles, the ones we used in Africa. We'll need you to porter our supplies, if that's all right with you."

"After all," Hampton added quickly, "I'm certain you're more than willing to pitch in to deserve your fee."

"A hunerd dollars, right?"

"Perhaps even more. A bonus! But we do expect you to cooperate and assist us as we require. Agreed?"

Velmer nodded. "Oh, I certain do. You gents are

decent fellers, and I'll promise we'll git that prize tro-phy. Bet on that." He eyed the jug on the table. "What about the liquor? You want it brung along with us?"

"No. Leave it here," Bryce said. "Because in a day or so you'll be celebrating your pay, and extra." Yoolee caught his smirk in the flickering yellow light. "A man can't celebrate dry."

Velmer shook his head. "Not hardly." He leaned a step closer to the men. "By the way, not a word to nobody around these parts about all the cash money I'm to get paid. Some of our local swampers can turn jealous and poke up mischief."

"No one will know," Bryce said.

Someone blew out the candle and they all left. Not very quietly. Outside, one of the hounds barked at the pair of strangers until a foot, probable Velmer's, kicked her to a mere whimper. Then the three voices could no longer be heard.

Havilah nudged him. "Yoolee, what was all that noisy talking about? I don't guess I could catch any of it."

"Nothing. No trouble." Reaching over, he patted her shoulder. "What say we forget it all and go to sleep."

Silently he figured that Velmer Tharp was fixing to gulp a bitter taste of something a lot hotter than what was in that jug.

▲ Chapter 5 ▲

"Hark up."

When his mother spoke, Yoolee quit spooning up a breakfast of crowder peas and grits, and listened. So did Havilah. Off toward the pines where the high ground was solid enough to allow a double-rut road through the weeds, Yoolee could hear a motorcar engine laboring along in low gear. As it cut off, a familiar horn honked three times.

Wooga. Wooga. Wooga.

"That's Bib," their ma announced.

Underneath the shack, both hounds began to bark. As Yoolee and his sister dropped their wooden spoons to tin plates and jumped up from the table, Ruth Ann grabbed each one by the shoulder.

"Hold on. It's close to half a mile uptrail to where Bib leaves his machine. Too distant to allow the pair of you to roam lonesome." Pulling the twenty from the wall, she broke it open, made sure a shell was in the chamber, then clicked it shut. "I'm fixing to tag along."

In spite of their mother's warning, Yoolee and

41

Havilah ran ahead. They both knew where Bib's car usual parked when their uncle come to visit—just south of an enormous banyan tree.

As he reached a wide clump of prickly pear, Yoolee stopped to wait for his sister. "Hurry," he said. For once Havilah had nothing to say, being a bit too busy at breathing.

There was Bib, bending over alongside the Ford, wearing khaki pants and a bright red shirt. He was examining the left front wheel, one hand touching the tire. As Yoolee and Havilah ran up, he turned, cuffed back his cowboy hat, and held out his brawny arms, bending a grin instead of his backbone.

Yoolee, who reached their uncle first, received an easy punch and a hearty hug. Havilah, a few steps behind, got picked up and tossed high. She giggled in the sunlight.

"You two's growing like vines up a tree," Uncle Bib said.

It got Yoolee to smiling when he watched Bib hold Havilah so near that their faces touched. Bib closed his eyes as if holding her was Heaven.

"You need a shave," she told him. "Your cheeks be scratchier than a cactus." As his sister was getting tickled next to crazy, Yoolee pranced around like a little kid, aching for another sock. Or maybe Uncle Bib would rassle him on the brown blanket of pine needles next to the Ford.

It was then that Yoolee happened to notice that Bib hadn't come alone. There she be, a lady wearing a fancy dress and a floppy hat that looked too heavy for her head, climbing off the passenger seat. Her face sported a rainbow of colors that Yoolee reckoned she must've slapped on with a trowel. All this, plus a pair of silly shoes. The tall heels weren't much helpful because they were soon sinking into the black muck that lay beneath the pine needles.

"Oh," said Uncle Bib, waving to Ruth Ann, who was approaching with the shotgun, "this'n here is Mimosa May Sugarman. I call her Sugar a lot. Sugar, meet my kin: Yoolee Tharp and young Miss Havilah…and their ma, who's my kid sister. Ruthie, say hello to Sugar." He gave both women a squeeze.

"How do," Ruth Ann said.

"Pleased to meet your acquaintance," Sugar chirped out in a high, wee-bitty voice that ought to belong, Yoolee was thinking, to a cricket.

Havilah smiled up at Mimosa May Sugarman. "Uncle Bib's real name is Bible. Mr. Bible Alderkirk. But we say Bib for short. What do *you* call him?"

"A lot of things," Sugar muttered, uncorking one of her high heels out of the ground as though to show them all it was dirty.

When she scowled and yanked off the pump, Bib said, "Sugar, you might want to consider carrying your shoes and going barefoot."

"I got *stockings* on," she snipped, "as any *fool* can see."

"Yes'm," Yoolee said with a wink. "Havilah saw it."

Hav kicked him into a chuckle.

With sort of a ho-hum look on his face, Bib looked around. "Don't guess I see Velmer."

"He's working," Ruth Ann told her brother. "Took off in the night with two gentlemen hunters. From Miami, I believe they mentioned."

Pointing at the twenty his sister was holding in the crook of an arm, Bib said, "Strange he didn't take his shotgun. Miami guys, you was saying?"

Ruth Ann nodded. "Big shots. So they s'pose."

"One's name was Bryce," said Yoolee, "and the other gent got called Hampton. Do people really have funny names like that? Bryce and Hampton? Those names are even sillier than Havilah."

Hav doubled a fist, but Uncle Bib caught her before she could let it fly and tickled her back to peaceable. "Vel ought keep to home," Bib said, "and watch over these two handsome towhead children."

Ruth Ann touched his arm. "We're right thankful you come a few days early, Bib. And I'll explain why."

"Maybe I already know, sis. Just yesterday I happen to meet up Joonyer Cobb in Copeland. He's that fella who never fails to inquire about *you*." Bib nudged her. "When he was parking his patrol car, I took a notice of how the gun rack was so serious armed. Hefty caliber.

So he told me about that missing girl."

"Walton Baggitt," Yoolee broke in. "He ain't a girl. Walton's a boy, like me, only a lot bigger. He cut me a turkey call."

Resting a big hand on Yoolee's shoulder, Bib said, "Indeed, the Baggitt boy's absent. But more recent one of Till Maddux's kids got killed. A little girl, only seven. I believe Joonyer allowed that her name was Lottie."

"*No!*" gasped Ruth Ann. She hauled Havilah a step or two closer to where she stood.

Until now, Yoolee hadn't told anyone, not even Hav, about what he was pretty sure was a human leg bone, the one that Ladylove had been gnawing on beneath the shack. Here, in front of his mother and sister, he wasn't about to open up the subject. But later he'd corner Bib alone, display the bone to him, and hear what he'd have to say.

"We got a trouble situation," his mother was saying to her brother. "It's too horrible to think about or talk on. If I was a decent Christian woman, I'd git Velmer to rent a wagon and carry me across to the Maddux place to comfort poor Agnes June.

"Imagine losing a child thataway. I can just bet that woman needs some solace."

"Truly a shame," Bib said, stuffing his hands in his pockets like he was searching for something to say. "Yet it's maybe best if everybody sticks close to home. Sis, you oughtn't to let Velmer stray off at such a time.

He belongs here." He pointed at the gun. "And likewise that twenty."

"He thinks he's to git a hundred dollars," Yoolee said.

Bib looked at him. "From them two Miami characters?"

Yoolee nodded. "Late last night me and Hav heard 'em yapping away like air was free. They had a jug, which I s'pose made 'em all itching to whoopee." To his mother, he added, "Old Velmer didn't want you, or anybody else, to find out about the money he been promised."

"We to stand here all day?" Sugar asked. "I'm near fixing to faint with the vapors."

Uncle Bib didn't say anything right off. He just let out a sigh that sounded as though it'd been a gas pocket that was worrying his insides for a week.

"Can we go home?" Sugar asked Bib as she swatted a bug. "You told me it'd be only a quick visit, and then we'd go to see a movie-picture show."

Bib's answer was to open up the Ford's trunk and yank out a rifle. Yoolee had seen it once or twice before and recalled it was a Winchester. He'd ached all over to shoot it once, but his uncle claimed he was still too puny. However, as they all walked the trail from the motorcar to the shack, his uncle awarded Yoolee a real treat.

He got to tote Bib's rifle.

▲ Chapter 6 ▲

They all tumbled inside the shack.

Miss Sugar, so it seemed, was possible used to fancier digs and was turning up her nose as though it smelled something overripe. Elbows close to her sides, she appeared to Yoolee like she was afraid to touch anything and suspected that something might try to touch her. She was a nonstop griper.

All three females were talking at once, producing a continuous babble that seemed more sounds than words. A look on Bib's face stated that he didn't care to listen.

"Come on, boy," he said, mussing his nephew's hair. "Let's us menfolks take a stroll outside. A long drive behind the wheel makes a feller need to unkink."

Yoolee grinned.

These, he was thinking as the pair of them left the shack, were the sunniest times of his whole life, being with Bib.

They hadn't wandered very far when his uncle stopped to spy on a spider.

"Look at her. Now, that's magic, little nephew, the wondrous way she's weaving all that delicate basketry. Each strand is wet when it leaves her body. Notice how it glistens between them two low-growing spikes of horny palmetto. Diamonds of daylight. Ain't that a miracle to behold?"

Bib touched the spider with a gentle fingertip, making her flinch a bit, yet she didn't spook and run.

"When a spider starts a web," Yoolee asked, "how does she stretch that first length from one tree to another? Seems to me that'd be impossible."

"Easy," Bib said. "She merely waits for a windy day, climbs up a tree to however high she cottons the crest of her web to be, and lets fly a long, sticky strand out her rump. When it sticks to the second tree, the mare spider's got herself a tightrope to cross. The rest of her chores are hang-down simple. In my opinion, Mrs. Spider creates more'n just a flytrap. She engineers a work of art, something gracious to gaze at."

"In the sunshine," Yoolee said, "it's silver and gold, sort of like the coins of a pirate's chest."

"Right." Bib tapped his shoulder. "Nature is the true richness of Earth, and it's what makes us feel wealthy. Best part of all, it's free. Our world's a warehouse of goodness, boy."

Walking to higher ground, Yoolee and his uncle moved easier among the massive trunks of pine trees.

"They smell good," Yoolee said. "It's candy for your nose."

Head back, Bib looked away up high. "See all them bright berets of fresh needles, young and light green, eager to replace the old ones that git dropped down?" Moving the toe of a boot, he added, "Brown needles are fallen soldiers, but up yonder the new needles are fresh recruits."

They walked a few steps more.

Bib pulled a leaf off a moonvine. "Green's always been my favorite color. Yoolee, I'd probable guess that God has green eyes, or a green thumb."

"You mean like leaves and grass?"

"Exactly like so. For certain, green has got to be God's chosen color. Look everywhere. All of Florida is what shade?"

"Green."

"All I know about God Almighty," Bib said, "is that He honors us by allowing us folks all to witness nature. I've come to believing that nature is God's silent Scripture. It's perfection without preachery. Can you read, Yoolee?"

Yoolee shook his head. "No, sir. Mama sometimes says that I ought to learn and then help to teach Havilah. Can *you* read, Bib?"

His uncle smiled. "Not without specs. Yet I certain hanker for you to learn how."

"If you want, Uncle Bib, I'll learn. Walton Baggitt

can read. Or could, anyways. And also write."

Bib whirled the moonvine leaf's stem between his palms, making the leaf spin a green blur of a spot. "It ain't too pleasant," he said, "to accept a fact that somebody you know's now a fallen needle."

"Why did Walton Baggitt die?"

"Well, it was maybe just his time, Yoolee. Or perhaps he took careless." Bib pointed a finger at his nephew, and the leaf fell to the ground. "So it's important, these days, to mind whatever your folks advise. Havilah, too. Best ya both snug up close to home, leastwise until the…the menace is hunted and shot."

"Is that why ya brung the Winchester?"

"Truly be." Bib kicked out a leg. "Let's walk a bit farther. My old knees are still stiff from the Ford, and my hearing's a bit deaf because Mimosa May kept asking me the same question about every mile: *Are we there yet?*"

The two of them walked for a while in silence.

"Is she your sweetheart, Uncle Bib?"

"Yup." Bib chuckled. "Lucky for me, Sugar ain't too particular." He let out a long sigh to empty his lungs. "I certain do wish your blessed ma had been fussier and not settled for that there Velmer Tharp. Tried to warn her at the time. But dear Ruthie was only seventeen, and Velmer was the first fruitfly gent who courted her attention or give her trinkets."

Yoolee held quiet. Sooner or later he'd open up to

.elling him about his pa's habits. But to say any-
tu…ig right now would be doing fooly. Bib would eventual leave, and then Velmer might lick meanness on
his family. Spilling too much to Bib could work matters worse.

In a place where the pines began to thin stood a
solitary live oak, pushing all other forms of life away,
as though staking claim to its round pool of shade.

Yoolee bent to pick up an acorn, mostly green,
some of it yellow, with a round, creamy moon, a sharp
tit on the other end. He tossed it to Bib.

"The seed of life," his uncle said, holding up the
acorn. "A little grenade that, once buried, is fixing to
go off, to explode into a giant puffball of a tree like the
one now shading us."

It was a cinch for Yoolee to monkey up a low limb
and then straddle a thick branch close to the trunk,
riding it like a horse.

Squinting up at him, Bib said, "Well, you'll certain
be safe up yonder." His uncle looked in all directions.
"I do suspect there's awesome misery out there, closer
than we might realize. Maybe more folks are going to
meet up with it. And die."

"One of our dogs found a bone."

"Dogs'll do such," Bib said.

"But this be a human bone." Seeing the doubt on
his uncle's face, Yoolee added, "I seen a skeleton one
time, so I'm sure of what our dog was gnawing."

"Did you tell Ruth Ann about this?"

"No, sir." Jumping down from the giant live oak, Yoolee landed close to his uncle. "I just kept the secret inside so Mama and Havilah wouldn't fret."

Bib touched Yoolee's shoulder. "Ya done proper. Yet in a way I'm grateful you saw that human bone, if that's what it truly be, because it's an omen. A warning to take care. From here forward, best we stay on guard. Eyes open."

"Is trouble coming to us?" Yoolee asked.

His uncle sighed. "More'n we can handle."

▲ Chapter 7 ▲

Mimosa May Sugarman threw a purple fit.

Yoolee also observed her throwing both shoes at Bib when he announced that they were going to stay overnight. In a calm voice, his uncle took a stab at explaining: Because Velmer wasn't home, he couldn't righteous leave his sister alone with two children.

"That thing's also killed a half-growed bull," he told his lady friend. "Ripped it into hide, horns, and raw meat."

"Who reported that?" she asked. Her plum heart-shaped lips were all puckered up into what looked like a knot on the north end of a sausage.

"Joonyer."

"Joonyer Cobb tells stories all over Collier County just to pump up how necessary he is to the taxpayers." Sugar stomped her foot. "I want to go home, you hear, Mr. Bible Alderkirk? Best you drive us back right this minute, or I'll consider ending our friendship." She pointed a pink painted fingernail at Bib's chest.

It served her no good.

Uncle Bib and Mimosa May Sugarman stayed. Although it was cramping, Ruth Ann slept in the loft between Yoolee and Havilah, so's the two of them wouldn't whack each other all night, and gave her bed behind the tarp to Bib and his lady. But the arrangement didn't sweeten Sugar. She cussed out a few old favorites. Curled up on the cornhusk tick, Yoolee tried to remember some of the fresher phrases, the ones that sounded most colorful.

"Mama," Hav whispered when everyone had settled some, "I seen a face today. When Yoolee'd run ahead of me to meet Uncle Bib, I seen a face in the ferns."

"That's nice," Ruth Ann said.

Yoolee didn't heed whatever Hav was mumbling in her sleep. His sister was usual pretending all manner of odd objects. Mostly, he figured, they existed only in her mind. Yet as Havilah didn't drop off, he began to ponder whether there be any truth to her tale.

"A browny face," Hav was insisting, "and it had long white hair, like an old woman." After a breath, she added, "It didn't budge. But then soon's I blinked to see clear, that old face upped and gone. I wanted to tell Yoolee, but I was too spent of air from trying to chase after him."

"Go to sleep, Havilah," their mother said, sounding tired.

"I could show y'all the spot," Hav kept jabbering, "on account I'll remember exact where that old person was standing." She paused to scratch a bug bite. "Weren't no body there at all. Mere a face floating in fern."

Hav final hushed herself to a quiet and didn't offer up even one more peep.

Yoolee was awake early.

The sun was barely up when he sneaked down the loft ladder to find Uncle Bib's gun. It stood in a corner. He picked up the rifle again. It felt aplenty bulkier than the family four-ten. And more gun than the twenty-gauge. Behind the trigger loop, the Winchester had a lever that Bib used to cock another shell into the firing chamber. His arms shaking due to the rifle's weight, Yoolee held the butt against his right shoulder, pretending to aim it. Squinting his left eye shut, he stared through the v-notch along the steel barrel at the little bead above the muzzle. As his finger hooked around the trigger, he pressured it a mite, yet it refused to budge.

Taking aim at an earthen crock in the corner partly behind the cookstove, Yoolee tightened his finger on the trigger. It weren't about to give any ground, and...

WHAM.

Urine flooded his overalls.

The crock shattered into pieces, and a stink of gunpowder was so sickening that he'd liked to puke out supper, which had been a fried possum. His eyes watered like a pump tap and his ears were ringing so loud, Yoolee felt a might lucky. That way he didn't have to listen up to everybody yelling at him, pointing their fingers and reddening their cheeks.

Ruth Ann, with her hair hanging down, couldn't seem to decide whether to blame her son or her brother. Havilah cried. Miss Sugar was screaming at everybody in Florida, and maybe even the northern shores of Cuba. Bib merely shook his head.

Unable to hear any of whatever it was they all were hollering, and it appeared to be plenty, Yoolee just sat on the shack's gritty floor, also wet, held the Winchester, and rubbed his hurting shoulder.

It soon seemed, however, that his smiling at everyone didn't actual help a whole lot to soothe their ire.

In a minute or so, Havilah exchanged her wailing for laughter. She pointed, giggling at each of the three growed-up shouters as they took turns losing temper. Ruth Ann pinned up her hair and began to crack eggs into a black cast-iron skillet, the one she always called a spider. Much to Yoolee's surprise, Sugar offered to help. Ruth Ann thanked her and said there wasn't that much to do. So Miss Sugar started remortaring her face, using a series of tiny boxes, bottles, and tubes that might add up into dozens. Her eyebrow-junk kit, Yoolee noticed, contained a little brush no longer than a pinky finger.

It seemed to interest Hav.

Picking up the baby brush, Havilah used it to

slough out dirt from between her toes. This she continued to do until Miss Sugar caught her removing a
particularly generous clod of topsoil. Making a face
that could've curdled milk, Sugar snatched the brush
away from Havilah, then chucked it at Bib, who
merely ducked.

With every breath, Yoolee's hearing slowly
returned, enough to hear Uncle Bib suggest, "Let's
you and I wander outdoors. We'll tote the rifle along to
keep us company. If you don't object, Yoolee, I'll carry
it."

Once the pair of them helped themselves to a comfortable sit with their backbones leaning against the
trunk of a tawnberry tree, Bib pinched Yoolee's knee
enough to spur a giggle.

"Now then," he said in his easy voice, "seeing as
you earlier got curious, this'n here weapon is a model
fifty-three Winchester lever-action rifle. To my knowl-
edge, it's manufactured in three sizes. This one's the
most potent, their forty-four-forty. The forty-four part
means the bore. Though I ain't...excuse me...I *am
not* exact sure, Yoolee, I believe the last forty is forty
grains of black powder in each cartridge."

One by each, Uncle Bib pumped the lever underneath the stock, emptying the rifle tube that bellied
along under the barrel. Brass somersaulted all over.

"This tube'll hold six rounds," Bib announced,
picking up every one of the scattered brass objects.

"Six bullets?"

"Not quite right." Handing one to Yoolee, he said, "This is a cartridge. The round end, the butt, holds a cap, which primes the main powder charge. That explosive expels the slug—the bullet—from its brass casing and out the gun's muzzle." Bib smiled down at him. "By the way, what's your shoulder feel like?"

"Good," Yoolee lied, not wanting to admit that he was feeling somewhat mule-kicked.

"From now on, Yoolee Tharp, you best stick to using the four hundred and ten, leastwise for a few more years. By then, maybe your shoulder'll abate its throbbing."

"I'm sorry, Bib."

"You dang ought to be." He cracked a grin at Yoolee. "Aw, it's all right. Nobody got winged. But in the future, before you start messing around with a gun, ask permission of a grownup, and also learn from him if it's loaded. Then check yourself to make certain." His big hand mussed up Yoolee's hair in a gentle way. "It would cut you a hurt if'n you wounded Hav or your mother."

Yoolee thought a moment. "I'd feel dingy if I actual smacked a bullet into any one of us."

Even, he was thinking, Miss Sugar.

▲ Chapter 8 ▲

Inside the shack, Yoolee noticed, his mother and Miss Mimosa May Sugarman seemed to need nobody else to join their never-end talking. Mostly at female matters. Or the shortcomings of Uncle Bib.

Earlier, Sugar's mood had soured enough to pickle beets. But when she realized that Bib aimed to tarry and not leave, Sugar rolled up her sleeves and shared in the housework. Using a broom, she certain rearranged the dust.

"At home," Sugar explained to Ruth Ann as she shook out a rag, "whenever I'm annoyed with Bib, *I clean.*"

Both women laughed.

Yoolee couldn't quite believe it when the two ladies ordered him, his little sister, and Uncle Bib out from underfoot.

"Youngsters," said Bib, "let's retreat outside and go rambling, the good ol' three of us."

That sounded all right to Yoolee. Havilah, however, begged off going, and told their uncle why: "Soon as

Miss Sugar takes a nap like she said she'd do, I'm fixing to empty her big pocketbook and try on some of her funny face paint."

Bib laughed to split a gut. "Havilah, honey," he told her, "I honest can't wait to see your face...and then see Sugar's."

So there be only a pair of them, himself and Bib, which suited Yoolee dandy fine. They'd best walk away from the shack at a rapid rate, Bib said, before his lady friend could fuss up another feud. Or blow a garter. He was still chuckling at his niece's scheme.

"That sis of yours," he said through a grin. "Havilah's a little red-hot spark that'll dance on gunpowder."

As they tramped through a patch of berries that sported white blossoms and purple fruit, Yoolee asked Bib what they were. "Elderberries," his uncle said. "Safe enough to chew and swallow, but keep clear of the leaves. They're poisonous."

There were plenty of berries to eat, so they had at 'em, as Bib put it, munching away until juices trickled from their chins, and their mouths were circled by purple. In the mood to talk, Uncle Bib explained a bit about boars and how, except for their rut season when the sows were in heat, the males stayed with other males. A bunch of boars, Bib claimed, was usual called a drift or a sounder.

Circling back in the direction of the shack, they

talked a bit about deer and bear, looked for tracks but didn't find any. Only a few droppings of deer pellets.

It was a long hike.

"Well," Bib said to Yoolee after several hours, "I'm about starved for more of Ruth Ann's cookery, so let's point to home."

"Okay by me," Yoolee said. "But I'd sure cotton to hear more stuff about boarhogs. What do they look like when they're little?"

"Well, though the mature hogs are black or reddish brown, they gradual turn gray as they age. Their youngsters are mostly brown, with sort of chipmunk stripes that run head to rump. The tails are straighter than a stove poker, not curly, and always tufted at the end."

"What's tufted mean?"

Fingers extended, Bib held up a hand. "Like so. A tuft is a soft, puffy ball, like the bloom on a thistle." He grinned down at Yoolee. "Come to think, there ain't actual nothing that's soft about a boarhog. They all got hides of steel. Too thick for most bullets to penetrate."

Upon returning to the shack, both Yoolee and Uncle Bib were surprised to find the liquor jug a mite closer to empty and Miss Sugar a gulp or two fuller. Ruth Ann was sober and sewing. Havilah, her face plastered with Sugar's cosmetics, lay asleep up in the loft.

"Wahooooo!" whooped Sugar at the sight of Bib. "Looky who's come home to assist us womenfolk to cook supper. Here he is, folks, Mr. Bible Alderkirk, best known as the champeen toastmaster."

"Aw, now, Sugar," Bib pleaded with a wince, "you ain't gonna tell that toaster story again, are ya?"

"No, not me," said Sugar, and waded smack into telling it. "Never before," she said, "had I ever seen a man somehow slip a necktie down into the slot of an electric toaster. Bib's tie busted into flame all the way up clear to his Adam's apple." Sugar slapped her thigh. "Then he tried to throw his toaster out the kitchen door."

"How far did he throw it?" Yoolee asked.

"Not very far. The toaster was still plugged to a extension cord and into the wall socket, so it whipped around his neck a couple of loops. You know, like a yo-yo."

Yoolee's smile was beginning to hurt because he was laughing so hard at poor Bib. "Did it put out the fire?"

Sugar shook his head. "Nope. His necktie was still burning. So a no-count buddy of his who was visiting tossed a full dipper of water at him. As the water dunked into the toaster, which was still plugged in, y'all should've seen the electric show Bib put on. Blew out every light in the house except the toaster sparks."

Ruth Ann and Sugar were clinging to each other to

keep from falling down, because they both were laughing so loud.

Bib looked aching to be somewheres else.

Holding his belly, Yoolee was rolling around on the shack's floor, giggling fit to bust because the humor was hurting so dreadful funny. "Stop," he groaned. "My ribs can't take it no more."

But Miss Sugar wouldn't quit. Her storytelling shifted into high gear. She was having so much fun at Bib's expense that she could barely whisper.

"Folks," she said, "I just wished you could've seen it. The front of Bib's shirt was a regular Fourth of July fireworks display." Miss Sugar paused for a breath. "Let me tell you, when it comes to helping out around a kitchen, especially entertaining, my sweet ol' Bib's just another Mr. P. T. Barnum."

"Oh," said Ruth Ann, "how I would love to have been there to witness that circus act."

"Believe me," said Miss Sugar, "you'da enjoyed the entire show. Come visit us sometime, and our clown will probable do it all again." She gave Bib a gentle little kiss on his forehead. "You know how he cottons to show off."

Up to this point Yoolee's sister had kept quieter than a midnight mouse, but then Havilah spoke up in her little squeaky-mouse voice.

"Bib, you toasted everything but the bread."

▲ Chapter 9 ▲

Everyone bit into breakfast.

It was the following morning, and Bib's lady friend had insisted that she was too hung over to take nourishment. But when the eggs, biscuits, and grits got to the table, Yoolee noticed Miss Mimosa May Sugarman was holding down the first seat. For five people, there were six biscuits in the tray, and Sugar's was the only gullet to surround two. Yet she did pitch in to earn her keep, helping Ruth Ann clear the table and scrub the skillet. Yoolee heard the dogs barking. Needless to say, neither Possy nor Ladylove charged out from under the shack. As usual, they stayed put and whined.

The goat bleated a few times as Bib opened the door to give a look outside.

"It's Hacksaw Hix," he said.

Just as his uncle spoke, Yoolee was hearing two strange dogs, but their growlings weren't at all like those the two Tharp dogs usual made. To Yoolee's ear, they certain sounded like a brace of animals that would attack anything or anybody. Again the Tharp dogs whimpered.

"Best you contain them two," Bib advised the visitor, "or they'll like to rip these lazy mutts into particles."

With a nod, Mr. Hix turned to his dogs and softly spoke only one word. "Still." The animals' eyes stayed glued on their elderly owner. As Yoolee watched, he was quick deciding that he wouldn't at all cotton to harming that particular gent or venture a hostile step in his direction. Not with those toothy lookouts.

"You got a vicious brace of hounds," Bib said. "I don't guess either of them two is fond of the Tharp family."

Mr. Hix spat. "Now that ain't exactly so. A few times I've allowed your little ones to pet both my dogs. No bother. Happens to be a whiff of Velmer they dislike. Were he to near one, Kicker or Cain might just remove Velmer's manly enthusiasm."

"For that, I'd buy a ticket to watch." Bib laughed. "You already ate, s'pose. Maybe we could persuade a cup of coffee from Ruth Ann. How about?"

"I didn't come for a handout."

Looking at Mr. Hix, Yoolee saw a tore shirt, rag-bottom pants belted by a knotted rope, and muddy boots. On his head was a floppy hat, once white, now a collection of stains. People claimed that Mr. Hacksaw

Hix was closing in on eighty, maybe more, but the old hermit was too cantakerous to die. At the offer of coffee, he never took a friendly pace forward. Instead, he stood as if ready for trouble, a knife at his hip and a shotgun in his hand, aimed down. In a sense, Yoolee thought, Mr. Hix looked like kin to his dogs.

When Bib left the shack to greet their neighbor, Yoolee followed. He hadn't seen Mr. Hix in a spell, and company usual had a way of bringing news.

The two men shook hands.

"Well," said Bib, "seeing as you didn't actual arrive here for groceries, what brings ya?"

Mr. Hix scratched hisself. "Nowhere near young as I used to be. Can't hear or see like years ago. So I'm recruiting someone to hunt alongside. By chance you bring a rifle? All I got is this here scatter." He raised the shotgun and then lowered it. "Might not be enough for what's ahead. That cussed critter's killed somebody dear to my heart."

"Who?" Bib and Yoolee both asked.

"You won't believe it when you hear. Happened just yesterday." Mr. Hix went on, "And I knowed him since he was a youngster. Seen him grow up to over three hundred pound. His name was Trace Jessup. Most massive man in the county. Stood tall, six and a half foot. His upper arms were burly as hams. But when I found him..."

Mr. Hix shook his head.

"What happened?" Bib asked him.

"Boar. After that hog'd tore poor Trace apart and chawed away his middle, it left prints in the muck. Not paw marks. Ones I spotted be cloven, you know, a forked hoof like Satan's, and close to the measure of a cow. Weren't a bear or panther. And a bull don't eat no meat."

Bib nodded. "For certain it's a boar."

"Best you tell Velmer to keep a tether on his family, or he'll be lacking one. Whenever a boarhog goes insane, it'll not do usual. Craves all kinds of blood. Animal or human."

Hearing what Mr. Hix was saying made Yoolee Tharp's spine go cold, like he wanted a blanket around him, one that would keep him out of sight.

"Velmer's not home," Bib said. "Seems he decided to stray off with a couple of Miami gentlemen. I guess they offered Vel a handsome price if they take a trophy head. Don't know which direction they headed."

Yoolee took a step forward. "In the night I was sort of listening to their big talk," he said. "Their names were Bryce and Hampton."

Mr. Hix spat. "Chances are, them three don't have a clue to whatever they're chasing, and not a one of them could locate his butt with both hands." He squinted at Yoolee for a breath. "Bryce and whatty?"

"Hampton."

"City fellers. Doubt either one's seen any tuskers parading along Miami Beach."

"Well," said Yoolee, "by the fancy way they was speaking, I didn't s'pose they come from around here parts."

"Bible," said Mr. Hix, "I don't know if'n I got the right to ask ya to hunt alongside me and make you abandon these people. But to be honest about it, I don't relish trying to tackle that critter by myself. I ain't that lonesome for pain."

"Maybe you ought to pack on home," Bib cautioned him, "and forget any notion you got as to baiting that beast."

"Can't."

"Why not?"

Mr. Hix looked away.

"Well, one night years ago, I got partial to Adele Hardesty before she married Roy Franklin Jessup. So, in a sense, Trace could've been *my* boy. I just might be Trace Jessup's daddy."

"A matter of conscience?" Uncle Bib asked.

"Sure is. Were I to hightail off, I wouldn't be able to sleep at night." Mr. Hix nodded at his hounds. "My dogs know there's something gnawing my mind. Sometimes they stare at me like they're fixing to ask what. To sum it, tracking down that monster be plenty matterful." He sighed. "Trouble is, I dasn't do it alone."

"Mr. Hix…"

"Call me Hacksaw, or Hack. I'm comfortable to it."

Bib smiled. "Hacksaw, may I please ask you to return here tomorrow, early morning?"

"Why tomorrow?"

"Because there are a few other people involved," Uncle Bib said, placing a hand on Yoolee's shoulder. "To be exact, there's five of us here. By tomorrow, if Velmer comes home, I'll be able to hunt with you."

"Enough," Mr. Hix said without smiling. "I'll report early." As he turned around and started to leave, his hounds hurried to heel, tails wagging high and anxious. But then he twisted back to face Bib again. "I got a request," he grunted.

"What is it?" Uncle Bib asked.

"If we hunt after that hawg," Mr. Hix said, pointing at the dogs beneath the house, "let's not even consider including those two excuses."

▲ Chapter 10 ▲

Yoolee and Hav were huddled under the shack.

It was usual a fair-to-decent hideaway from grownups because it was dark, quiet, and cool. The two best reasons were Possy and Ladylove. Both hounds were warm, silky soft, and perfect for pillows.

Yoolee's head rested on Possy's flank, Hav's on Ladylove's.

"We'll git cooties in our hair again," Havilah said, like it was news. "And then we'll have to do what we did last time, to get rid of them biters."

"Yeah," said Yoolee, "but it works. Just lie down right careful near a mound of fire ants and allow a few to creep all over us, and they'll nab every tick. Mama does that sometimes to rid our blanket of bedbugs."

Up above, Miss Sugar was on the warpath again, throwing things at Bib and screaming. Her temper was so sharp that Yoolee wondered how Uncle Bib could tolerate her company for even a day, say nothing of portering her along in the Ford on a road trip. Yet the two people did seem to favor each other. Sometimes, they held hands when looking up at the moon. Perhaps a hot scrap was their favorite sport.

Hav giggled. "She called him a sorry word."

"I heard it."

"What's it mean, Yool?"

Yoolee knew. Yet he wasn't about to let Havilah in on the secret. She was a girl and much too young to learn cheeky language.

"Sugar," he heard Bib warn, "now don't you throw that."

Ker-bonk!

"She certain throwed it," Hav said, "whatever it was."

Sugar kept stoking her temper close to overboiling until Bib went outside and hung a hammock between two black mangrove trees. A person could sag into it and enjoy a peaceful nap without a dog for a pillow.

Sugar wasn't buying.

"Come on now, darlin'," Bib pleaded. "A comfortable rest will soothe your nerves and you'll forget about our having to tarry here."

After another storm of groans and complaints, sprinkled with cussing, Miss Mimosa May Sugarman tried to mount the hammock, with Uncle Bib helping. It certain was a haul. Crawling closer, Yoolee and Havilah could spy on her, noticing that feet up and shoes off, her chubbiness sagged a big bulge in the hammock. She filled it like a breeze to a frigate.

"Look at there," Hav whispered. "Miss Sugar's got a tiny little hole in the toe of her stocking. Let's shock her with a *boo,* Yoolee."

"No, not quite yet. We'll wait until she's sleeping, and then I got us a juicier idea."

They didn't have long to wait. Temper had a way of tiring people out, so before Yoolee could count to a hundred, Sugar had quit her fidgeting and eased into slumber.

"Havilah, here's what we do. When I give the signal, you yank Ladylove's tail, and I'll do likewise to Possy. Ready?"

"Ready," Hav said. "I got a purchase on it."

"Now!"

Yoolee yanked, and as Havilah did the same, both hounds let out a sharp bark. The sound sent Miss Sugar rigid as though she'd took a jolt of voltage. The hammock, perhaps also frighted, seemed to react by tossing the lady friend like a skillet turns a pancake. She flipped like a flapjack. Florida trembled into an earthquake when hit by that big bag of Sugar. She was a load. Trying to get up and run, Sugar appeared to get tangled in the hammock ropes and let loose some unpasteurized English.

The hubbub fetched Bib outdoors. "What's wrong?" he asked as if he couldn't notice the mess

Miss Mimosa May Sugarman had made of herself and the hammock. He helped her to stand.

"Yool," Hav whispered, "there's a sleepy ol' hornet crawling on the ground near Miss Sugar's toe. The one with the stocking hole."

Yoolee saw Sugar move her foot and then place it on the hornet. She didn't appear to notice. He wondered if that hornet was maybe too lazy to sting. It wasn't.

"Yeeeeeooooowwww!"

Yoolee was impressed that Miss Sugar could dance so spirited a jig using only one foot and holding the other. Soon as her breath wore out, she managed to stand still in order to abuse Bib.

"Look," Hav said, "the hornet is alive. It's on her foot."

Havilah was right. Yoolee could detect a tiny brown bug on her stocking, the one that featured a toe hole.

Bib got his fancy lady settled into the hammock a second time, then retreated inside the shack. Yoolee could hear him talking to Ruth Ann. Something about danger. Meanwhile, the hornet now seemed to be seeking a hiding place of its own, away from all the hubbub and hollering. It merely inched along the stocking until it stopped to inspect the hole. Perhaps it was waiting for Sugar to go to sleep again, which she appeared to be doing, if snores were any proof. Then, maybe to escape, the hornet decided that the stocking hole offered a handy nest. In it went.

"I gotta see this," Hav whispered.

"Hush," Yoolee hissed at her. "You'll wake up Bib's lady friend, and then our uncle will be down on both of us. I'm in enough soup because of his gun this morning."

Sugar began talking in her sleep. "Bib, you best remove your sneaky hand from my leg, or Hell won't hold me. You hear?" She opened an eye to look for him. "Bib? Who's crawling up inside my stocking?"

Sugar produced a scream that could peel varnish.

"Nobody with any brains," Yoolee told Havilah, "ever hollers at hornets. It sort of gits 'em upset."

By now Sugar was rolling around in the hammock, both legs kicking the air. The hornet was becoming a bit sick of the entire scene and disliked being slapped at. Bib, looking tired, came outside a second time to learn what the ruckus was all about.

"Now what's to bother?" he asked Sugar.

"It's a *bee!*"

"No, it ain't," Havilah blurted out before Yoolee could muffle her mouth. "It's a hornet."

"Them!" Sugar was yelping again and pointing underneath the shack at two children and the pair of dozing dogs. "*They* did it. It's all their fault!"

Yoolee knew that a bee stung only once. A hornet, however, could plant its sharp old stinger into flesh as often as it chose. This hornet seemed to choose often. Still in the hammock, Miss Sugar was tossing, twisting, and yelping, rapidly becoming tangled in all the cords. Bib couldn't quiet her to save himself. And it was certain plain that the hornet didn't enjoy being inside Sugar's stocking, even though there sure was a lot of leg up yonder for a target.

Uncle Bib was efforting to hold his lady friend down so's he could locate the hornet, as any gentleman would. But a tussle with Sugar looked to be less pleasant than trying to bulldog a rodeo steer. At every sting she was blaming poor Bib.

The hornet final flew off.

"What's funniest of all," Yoolee told Havilah, "is that Possy and Ladylove slept throughout the entire business."

▲ Chapter 11 ▲

Velmer Tharp arrived near naked.

To Yoolee, he didn't actual look that way, on account his white hairy body was so coated with blood and dirt. Both dogs were whining as the battered man came staggering through the open doorway.

Confused, his mouth kept moving without saying even a word, only the groans and gaspings of a person in heavy pain.

As the blood wasn't red, Yoolee guessed it had been drying on his pa for a spell. There were no fresh wounds. Velmer's hands were holding his belly as though he was afraid of coming apart. Bib caught him as he fell. He laid Velmer down on the food-stained planks of the eating table, his head on wood and boot-less feet dangling down the far end.

"Almighty," said Uncle Bib. "Almighty God, what-ever in the deuce happened to you, Vel? Can ya speak?"

Velmer Tharp's mouth made noises that seemed to start in a head gone crazy and then emptied out between lips that were cracked and puffy. His chin, covered with several days' growth of beard, trembled without cease. Raising his head, Velmer attempted to check his privates, trying to decent himself.

Ruth Ann pulled Havilah away.

"I gotta see," Hav said.

Bib quickly covered Velmer's lower body by removing his own shirt to do it. Being covered seemed to settle old Velmer some, and his mouth quit opening and closing.

"Ruth Ann," Uncle Bib said in a calm voice, "please fetch me a bowl of warm salty water and some clean rags. Nothing that's too rough. Before anything else, we best take a gander at what's beneath all the blood and soil."

For some reason, Velmer didn't cotton to washing hisself very often or shaving. Right now, he seemed to be taking to it even less, putting up a fight, trying to knock a rag from Uncle Bib's hand.

"Ruth Ann, you and Sugar had best assist me and stand on opposite sides of the table, to shackle his arms." The ladies helped out. But when Velmer began to kick up, Bib said, "Yoolee, hold his legs. Stanchion his feet underneath your armpits and force your pa to quit battling."

Yoolee grabbed one foot, but the other one tried to kick his face. Nonetheless, he managed to take a firm purchase on both of his pa's skinny ankles and hang tight.

"I got 'em, Uncle Bib."

"What can I do?" Havilah asked.

"Here, sweetheart." Bib handed her a bloody rag. "Bring me a clean cloth and then go rinse this one out. Keep 'em coming to me until your daddy's cleaned up proper."

Yoolee almost snorted. *Proper* was hardly a trait that anybody'd use to describe Velmer Tharp. Mean, ornery, sneaky, greedy: They'd be better-fitting words. Add another to the list: drunk. Yoolee wasn't too Christian to think such, but here lay a gent who'd take pleasure in somebody else's pain. Now he was swallowing a hearty taste. That wasn't bothering Yoolee a whole lot, excepting he wasn't too proud of himself for thinking so unforgiving.

Bib bathed Velmer.

Miss Sugar had turned away, refusing to stare. Nevertheless, she maintained a grip on Velmer's forearm, doing her part. Yoolee had to give her honest credit for gumption. His mother held the other arm, her face blank, as though she didn't rightly give a hoot if old Velmer took to healing.

"Ruth," said Bib, "he'll need sewing. His gut's tore up ugly." Pressing a rag to Velmer's middle, he said, "I'll take his arm if you go thread a needle."

Ruth Ann returned, pushed a length of white thread through a needle's eye, knotted it, and started on the first stitch.

Velmer shouted a bad word.

It didn't stop Ruth Ann. Not much did, Yoolee was thinking as he watched her work. Her hands were small, yet they appeared to handle any task in a strong way, as if there was might inside her somewhere, ready to spew out like spite from a cornered coon. He had a hunch, as he watched Hav wringing out pink water from a bloodied rag, that his sister was certain cut from the same sturdy stuff. Only Havilah had a passel more to say, and usual spoke it out.

Velmer swore. Not just once.

Over and over he grunted his pigsty words. Ruth Ann didn't approve of cussing, so at every one of his outbursts, her needle pricked and punctured old Velmer's hide. It was, Yoolee was guessing, his mother's way of ordering him to clam up.

The sewing took ample time. It was hardly a pleasant sight to watch, and the smell of Velmer's body about soured every nostril in the shack. The man's stink would gag a maggot.

Sugar sort of retched. "I apologize," she said softly, "but I'm terrible afraid I'm going to get sick."

"No," Bib told her in a firm voice, "you're *not*. Just stand there and perform your job like the rest of us. You can see what begs doing, so keep helping instead of hinder. If you can't bear to watch, close your eyes." His voice softened. "So far, Sugar, you're doing proud."

"I am?"

Uncle Bib nodded and then leaned closer to kiss her hair. "In fact, because you're being such a decent helper, I'll present you with a ree-ward."

"What is it? If it's another meal of squirrel meat or that gritty coquina chowder, I pass, in every sense of the word."

"No. Not that."

"Tell me."

"Endure it, Sugar. On account this surprise that's in store for you will require some patience. More'n a mite."

"Dang you, Bib. You always have to rascal everything."

"Hush," Ruth Ann said quietly. "All your bickering don't make sewing no easier. I'm near to done, and I'll finish faster if people don't fret me with fussing."

Sugar said, "Please excuse me."

"You're excused," Hav piped in. "Uncle Bib, what's the surprise going to be? I want to know too. Is it only for Miss Sugar?"

"Nope. In a way it's a gift for all of us. A slice of goodwill. Might be fun to make y'all wait, seeing as everyone's so itchy to find out."

"I can't stand it, Bib," said Ruth Ann as she was biting a thread. "Either tell us or keep mum about it. I agree with Sugar. You have a bad habit of hinting at something and then tormenting. You're a tease and a torture, Bible Alderkirk, and you always were."

Bib grinned. "Me?"

"Amen," said Miss Sugar.

"Yes. I'd like to stitch your mouth," said Ruth Ann. "And then, while I'm at it, sew up Velmer's and maybe a few other places."

"Okay," said Bib, "I'll tell Sugar her surprise."

"What is it?" she asked. "I could surely use a gooder."

"You," Bib told his love bug with a wide smile, "are going to abide here as an honored guest for a few extra days to help nurse Velmer."

Ruth Ann covered Havilah's ears.

▲ Chapter 12 ▲

Velmer slept most of the day.

Finally, upon reopening his eyes, he didn't try to sit up. His hand kept touching his belly as if to check whether he was still whole instead of in tatters.

Yoolee stared at his pa in confusion, aware of both hatred and pity. Velmer Tharp acted like a brainless fool sometimes; at others, like an unfeeling bully. Clenching his fists, Yoolee felt he could stand tall enough to take any insult or beating that his father could dish out. What hurt deepest was Velmer's sneaky spying on his little daughter, plus the abusing of his woman.

Yoolee was still too puny to attempt getting even on Velmer. Not quite yet. He'd have to hold patient and thicken.

"My day will come," he told himself, turning away from his father, "and Velmer Tharp will reap his due."

His uncle was outside having a pipe on the gray wooden stoop and sort of studying the evening clouds. Yoolee joined him.

"Uncle Bib," he asked, "how come our hounds are keeping to home? They usual scamper off soon as the sun sinks. They're still hunkered under the house."

"Dogs are uncanny. They smell more'n spoor or scents, boy. Right now both of those animals are realizing that something's wrong inside. Maybe they inhaled a whiff of your daddy's blood loss and perhaps even nosed a taste of its cause."

"They know what did it? I'd sure say no. They probable can't, because us *people* don't know what happened."

"I do."

"You honest do?"

Bib relit his pipe, sat on the porch's edge, then lifted one knee for his hands to hug. "Well, while you and Ruth Ann and Havilah were out gathering up stove wood, Velmer managed a few words of explaining. He was still shaking."

"Was it the boarhog?"

Bib nodded. "Seems like those two men from Miami merely used Velmer Tharp to do their dirt work. Dirty and dangerous. Somehow they located that monster, heard it, but couldn't see it because of the thick vegetation. Velmer said he could smell the critter. Well, they ordered him to wade into the cover and spook it out. He balked. So they pointed their rifles at him, told him if'n he refused to go, they'd cut him down and bury him alive."

90

"He told you all that?"

"He did, Yoolee. Inside, on that cot, we have a man who's near to insane with fear. Unarmed, he had to face absolute terror of the most ferocious kind, an aging and enormous boarhog that's possible lost all reason. The thing attacked just as he hollered for help. Velmer claimed the boar roared louder than any bear."

"Golly." Yoolee paused to wonder. "But what happened to Bryce and Hampton? Didn't they shoot?"

"My guess is they heard the commotion and took themselfs afar. I doubt they lingered to squeeze off even a single round. And I'd be some surprised if Bryce and Hampton were their real names."

Yoolee recalled how the two men sounded late that night, full of whiskey and even fuller of brag. "Pa got took in, Uncle Bib. That hundred dollars was mere a come-on, like bait for a foolish fish."

His uncle smiled at him.

"You have a decent mind, Yoolee Tharp. Even though you're half-growed, you can reason." His hand touched Yoolee's hair. "Between your ears, we got some sensible smoke coming out of this little factory."

"Pa got greedy."

"Sounds like." Bib slowly shook his head. "And poor Velmer is paying for his greed with groaning."

"How'd he bust loose of that critter?"

"Yoolee, I have no idea, except that Velmer was just plain lucky. Maybe the boar got distracted, turned away from Vel to take after the two dudes, and allowed your daddy to crawl away. Or bury hisself. He possible snuck into a hole inside a rotty log. Lord knows how long he remained hid, trembling in the dark and getting chawed by insects. His flesh all bit to pitiful."

"I'm glad," Yoolee wanted to say so loud the whole world might hear it. Yet he forced his mouth to stay closed.

There was so much poison inside him that he ached to puke it out. It made him feel like a rattler snake, loaded with venom and itching to strike. That, however, would be cowardly. Instead, he'd wait for the time to face Velmer direct. Perhaps, Yoolee was considering, he'd just up and forgive Velmer and let it all go. Forgiveness, his mother told him, might be more righteous than revenge. And more comforting.

"You're so quiet, Yoolee. Are ya cogitating?"

"A mite. More'n that, I'm sort of learning. Storing up. Then one of these years I'll turn able to use what's inside my brain."

Bib stared at Yoolee for a long moment. "You hate him, don't you? No need to fess up about it. I already know, from what Ruth Ann tells me. She knows. Feels it. Perhaps she's never said it out, Yoolee, but your ma's proud of you. Telling out ain't her way. Ruth Ann holds it inside her, as do you."

"The three of us might live better without him, Uncle Bib. He don't do for us. Only for hisself."

"I been sensing that for a number of years." Bib sighed. "But it didn't seem called for to interfere in my sister's life. None of my business. If'n matters here become unbearable bad, I always figured she'd report it to me. You see, Yoolee, your pa usual behaves whenever I'm here to visit."

"That's his way. Slicker than a garfish."

Havilah joined them on the porch.

"What you people talking on?" she asked.

Uncle Bib took her in his lap, horsing her up and down a bounce or two, and kissed her soft, cornsilky hair. "Not much, little niece of mine. What you been doing inside? Helping your ma?"

Hav nodded. "And know what? Miss Sugar actual brushed my hair with her good brush and said I'd someday turn pretty."

Yoolee snickered, and Havilah socked him.

"Also," she went on, "I been listening to Daddy. He tries to sleep, but then once his eyes close shut, he maybe dreams bad things. That makes him wake up with a jump and the jitters. If'n he sleeps, what hurted him begins to spook him all over again."

"That's right, lamb. Your pa's had a terrible fright. He probable thought he was going to be shot or eaten up alive. I hope you two children never have to see up close what Velmer seen. That'd scare any man."

Hav said, "It wouldn't scare you."

Bib smiled. "Oh, indeedy it would." He bounced

her again. "Let me tell the pair of you about fearing, so's you'll know what it be. Fear is a form of intelligence. Our mind is warning us of danger, advising us to take action. Or take cover. You know, to hightail and scamper to safety like an armadillo."

As Bib talked, Yoolee was thinking that his uncle appeared to be near a mountain beside Havilah. Five or six times bigger, probable twice the size of Velmer Tharp. Nothing in the wide world ought to frighten a man as brawny as Bible Alderkirk. What was it that Mr. Hacksaw Hix had said about Trace Jessup? Six and a half foot, biggest man in the county, yet that hog wounded him up to a sorry finish.

The thought made Yoolee sweat chilly.

"Bib, if that animal comes here to our place and tries to break in our door, what ought I to do?" he asked. "Shoot, I s'pose. I've shot our trusty four-ten more'n twice, ain't I, Hav?"

Covering her ears, she said, "It makes too loud a bang. And it smells sour." Pinching her nose, she added, "I don't guess I'd want to shoot it even a one time."

Knocking the ashes from the pipe, which had already burnt out and was lying on a plank, Uncle Bib thrust it into his shirt pocket. Then he hugged both Yoolee and Havilah.

"Tomorrow," he said, "I'm to hunt along with Mr. Hix. But everything here'll be all right. Providing"—

he lifted a finger—"y'all do how I tell ya."

With her little arms around her uncle's thick neck, Havilah said, "I don't want you going away."

"Nor do I." Bib sighed. "Ruth Ann knows where my keys to the Ford are if I don't drag myself home alive. She'll ask Joonyer Cobb to drive Miss Sugar back to town. Before she leaves, I want you both to give Sugar a hug for me." Bib briefly closed his eyes. "Inside, she's a tender woman. At times, sort of brittle. That's why she blows off temper: to defend her deep feelings. Sugar doesn't resent you children. She just never got blessed with any of her own."

Hearing his uncle speak soft, and so gentle, made Yoolee Tharp think a lot more kindly of Mimosa May Sugarman.

▲ Chapter 13 ▲

Mr. Hix returned.

Outside it was still middle night, and the dogs were whining. As Yoolee opened his eyes, he could see that Uncle Bib had lit a lantern and was pulling on a shirt. His shadow was a black giant on the wall.

Miss Sugar mumbled in her sleep. Bib glanced at the sound and halfway smiled.

He was dumping a few extra cartridges into his pockets. The brass was twinkling little sparks of amber in the lantern light. Yoolee could hear Mr. Hix ordering Kicker and Cain to stay silent, but the dogs sounded eager, probable suspecting that a hunt was about to hatch.

Unbarring the door, Uncle Bib opened it and tossed a brief wave to the darkness. "Howdo," he called softly to Mr. Hix.

"Yup. You ready for that hog?"

"About," Bib said in a low voice. "Let's not you and me rouse everybody. I'll be along in a shake."

Mr. Hix grunted his impatience, and one of the

dogs let out a howl as if to say he already smelled a scent and was itching to track. Peeking out through a crack between two slabs, Yoolee could see one of Hacksaw's dogs dancing his front paws.

Blowing out the lantern, Bib left.

Havilah was no longer asleep. She now began to tug at the back of Yoolee's hair, yet he kept his eye to the narrow slit to find out which direction the hunting party was headed. They seemed to move north.

His hair was hurting. "Quit it, Hav."

Havilah punched him.

Her doing this always made Yoolee grin because it didn't rightful hurt. It was only Havilah's way of saying that they were beyond just a brother and a sister. They were pals. That was cause enough not to hit her back, yet Yoolee had another reason. He wanted to get Havilah quieted again so he could carry out his caper.

"Go back to sleep, Hav. Please do."

"All right. But come morning, I owe you another sock. You want to know why?"

Yoolee sighed. "Why?"

"Because you're so piggy at our peek-out place between them two planks. You never give *me* a turn at spying."

"I'm sorry, Hav. And I will let you uppercut me later, soon as it's light. A good hard one."

Eyes closed, his little sister nodded agreement. And already she was practicing at doubling up a fist.

Pretending to ease back to sleep, Yoolee Tharp felt quite awake. His brain was working away at a gallop, knowing that Havilah wouldn't be hitting him at all. He'd be gone. It wasn't a deciding of the moment. All day long he had plotted to trail after Uncle Bib and Mr. Hacksaw Hix and those hounds that looked as though they'd not retreat from the devil himself.

The plan made Yoolee smile.

On the other side of Havilah, their mother was motionless, the way she usual slept, too tuckered to get disturbed. In a minute or two, he'd crawl off the tick and down the short ladder, then sneak out the door. Last night, before going to bed with Hav, Yoolee had tested the floorboards to learn which ones set solid and which squeaked.

Trouble was, once he'd got hisself down to the floor, it was too inky black to count the cracks between boards, and this irked him to forgetting about the squeaking wood. To Yoolee's right, the rattle of wheezing breaths, plus the smell, warned him of old Velmer's whereabouts. One strong whiff of his pa made Yoolee wince. The man had a sickening scent, not too different from the rotted remains of a gator-bit turtle that had died nearby a week ago.

On tiptoe, standing at the two food shelves, Yoolee stuffed his mouth with cornbread. He chewed up a soft-boiled onion and cold grits left over from breakfast, and topped things off with a slab of sweet-potato pie. He seldom wore a shirt. Over his head he pulled on a raggy shirt he'd recent found that was too large, because it was Velmer's. It might serve to fend off bugs. At least the shirt was fresh washed and didn't stink of its owner.

"Now," he whispered, "for the twenty."

Long ago, Yoolee had learned where Velmer hid a supply of shotgun shells. Under a loose plank in the floor was a small box with a lid. Now, still unable to see, he felt for the shells. The green ones fit the four-hundred-ten. The larger shells were red, for the twenty-gauge. He took only three red ones.

As Yoolee was replacing the free plank to flat, it slipped out of his fingers and spanked into its slot with a loud *whack*.

"Hush up, Bib," Sugar moaned sleepily from the loft. "Still. Stay still and rest, my sweet lamb."

Yoolee froze. He thought he heard Ruth Ann mumble to Havilah. Then all darkened back to stillness.

His heart pounding, Yoolee managed to inch to the door, open it, sneak to the outside, and close the door behind him.

Once his feet met the ground, moonlight showed the sleep forms of Possy and Ladylove, awake and yawning, not bothering to stand. The two lazy hounds seemed about as interested in going boar hunting as they'd be in climbing a pine.

Yoolee moved north.

In his hand the twenty-gauge felt a lot heftier than the slender four-ten. This was a man's gun, hard and heavy. Its power seemed to be climbing right up his arm clear to his shoulder. To Yoolee's left, the frogs in the slough were croaking their usual nightly chorus, with the bugs singing along. One particular bug sounded pesky. It kept nagging a warning:

"Yoolee Tharp. Go back home.
Yoolee Tharp. Go back home."

Two hounds and two hunters had made tracks with a dozen feet that were pig-simple easy to follow under the starlight. Only when the moon ducked behind a cloud did the sudden gloom force Yoolee to bend closer to find the footprints. The familiar black shape ahead was merely his uncle's Ford, still parked, appearing to be asleep. As he passed it by, Yoolee reached out to touch a fender. For a brief moment, it made him feel nearer to Bib.

It was plain to see that his uncle and Mr. Hacksaw Hix had walked near the car. One of the dogs must have stopped to sniff a tire and then wet on it. Urine was shining against the black rubber.

"Hey there, Bib," he said to the Ford.

Wondering if he'd be able to keep tracking them, Yoolee forced his feet to a trot, the blanket of pine needles whispering little secrets to his bare toes as he ran.

Perhaps he should have worn boots, but as he didn't own any, such was impossible. His feet couldn't yet fill Velmer's. Then, he recalled, his pa had returned home without them, wearing mostly mud.

"Velmer, you'd be het-up angry if you knowed I'd borrowed your shotgun."

Beneath his feet the brown needles gradually yielded to wetter and blacker earth as the ground sloped down toward another slough. Yoolee had been here before, wading for frogs to gig. He remembered that he'd seen three kinds of mangrove trees. Black, red, and white. What was it that Uncle Bib had said about them? A few sacrificial leaves on every mangrove sucked in ocean salt from the brackish water until they'd suicide to yellow, die, and fall.

Saying the word aloud, even in a low whisper, coated Yoolee's flesh with goose bumps, making him question if he was doing foolish by following his uncle and Mr. Hix.

"Suicide."

▲ Chapter 14 ▲

Yoolee's eyes opened. Morning had finally come.

For several moments he blinked into the wet soft-ness of an early swamp, unable to recollect how he'd managed to snooze. Yet he recalled sitting and leaning against a tree to rest.

His back was hurting because his spine had been tight against the smooth gray trunk of a royal palm. Sitting had put his bottom to sleep, and both butts felt numb. As Yoolee budged, his body started to tingle as though trying to awaken. When he wiggled the toes of his right foot, they began to buzz into pinpricks.

Across his lap lay the scattergun. "You're here," he said, stroking the dented stock and trying not to fear it.

How strange to notice the dimples in its brown hardwood stock. There were things he'd never both-ered to behold whenever Velmer's gun was hanging in its usual position on the shack's inside wall. He wasn't allowed to touch it, say nothing about pulling it off its pegs. Had he done so, old Velmer would've put a belt buckle to his hide for sure.

Sudden screams jolted him fully awake.

A breath or two later, Yoolee realized it was only a raptor, of which there were plenty in the glades. At first, glancing up to see the black and white feathers, he thought the bird was a caracara. But no, because its nest was large enough to cradle a cow. There was a pair of eagles now, spreading their great wings and flapping away into the morning mist.

Had something disturbed them?

In a blink Yoolee Tharp turned and saw what had flushed the eagles. But it disappeared. *A face!* Exactly as Havilah had described, aged and tawny, with white womany hair hanging over the ears. A wrinkled face.

"A Calusa."

Memories of the early morning's darkness rushed into his mind. The fear of being alone, not knowing where he was, unable to locate Bib's tracks. Frozen in fright, he'd hid from a night that seemed to be so black and so big.

The thought crawled along his skin like cold worms.

But now he wasn't alone. The Calusa was watching him.

"Who are ya?" he yelled. "My name's Yoolee Tharp, and I got myself a shotgun. You hear?"

No answer.

Clicking the catch, he broke open the gun to make

sure a shell was in the chamber. It was. Although the red sleeve was seated forward out of sight, Yoolee could see the brass cap and even its little silvery center. Satisfied, he snapped the gun closed, hoping that the stranger would hear its warning.

Yoolee got to his feet, turning over in his mind what little he'd heard about the people of the Nation. He took comfort in presuming that the Calusa people weren't stirred up. He hadn't met many. The few he'd seen appeared a lot more peaceful than grumpy old Velmer Tharp, who didn't call anybody a friend.

Aware that he'd been leveling the shotgun at the mysterious face, Yoolee slowly raised the gun's muzzle, resting its butt to the earth.

"If you be watching," he said loudly, "I ain't fixing to hurt nobody or cut down. So you don't have to be afraid."

His echo melted into mangroves.

Rays of morning began to pierce the upper lace of palms and cypress as sunlight filtered down to chase away the night. A golden beam shafted to the earth to bless Florida. And to illuminate more tracks plain as day.

Yoolee felt brighter.

Looking up, he thanked the sun.

Trying not to make any noise, he tiptoed to where the tracks now lay, wondering if he was still being watched. Hurriedly glancing both ways, Yoolee saw nothing but greenery. At his feet the tracks now appeared to be easier to follow than the county road. His uncle's boots looked half again as large as those of Mr. Hix.

Turning to where he'd seen the face, he said, "I ain't afeared of you, Mr. Calusa person. So you can follow along with me if'n ya got a hanker."

There was no movement behind the brush or among the tree trunks. Not even a leaf fluttered. Yet Yoolee Tharp suspected that whatever he'd seen, it was the same face Havilah saw.

"Hav," he said, following the tracks north, "I certain do believe you now, girlie. You be telling us true about a strange face."

Gradually the land became more dried out, firmer beneath his feet, easier to tread on, and safer. Here an alert eye could spot a cottonmouth or diamondback and not be bit.

After an hour or so, it was a lead-pipe cinch to detect a place where both men had paused to rest. Beneath a tree. It was an ugly custard apple, rough-barked with small pointy leaves and a few soft apples fit only for grackles or squirrels. Most of them stood in water, yet this one was merely on wet land. Underneath, the scrub lay flattened in two places. One was large, where Bib had sat. Mr. Hix's seat was smaller.

Nearby, flies buzzed where one of the dogs had

emptied his bowels. The dog had tried to cover his drop with loose grass, but the flies hadn't been discouraged. The brown lumps looked fresh and wet, meaning that the four of them weren't far ahead.

Yoolee trotted on.

"That old Mr. Hix won't be going too fast, not at his age," he panted. "About every so often he'll have to pull up for a breather."

After another hour of jogging through the rising Florida heat, Yoolee began to guess that he was possible wrong. The old gent was keeping up steady. In fact, at the men's next resting spot only one of them had flopped down to flatten plenty of weeds. Yoolee noticed that while his uncle had rested, Mr. Hix had stomped a whole bunch of tracks as he paced back and forth, impatient to move ahead.

Yoolee grinned.

"Bully for you, ol'-timer."

Yoolee didn't stop for long. He pushed on, feeling the twenty-gauge grow heftier with every step. Perhaps it would have been brainier to bring the four-ten. At least he didn't have to tote Bib's big Winchester forty-four-forty. His right shoulder still held ample misery from the one time he'd fired that cannon.

His uncle didn't fly into a tantrum, even though it'd been plain to see on his face that he wasn't too pleased. Had it been old Velmer's rifle, well now, the

Tharp shack would have cooked in cussing and rage. All that, plus a belting.

As he walked along following the tracks, Yoolee tried to recall what Uncle Bib said one time concerning temper. A form of going crazy in the head, like madness.

Remembering, he could almost hear Bib's voice saying, "You can measure a man by the size of whatever turns him angry."

▲ Chapter 15 ▲

Voices?

Yoolee stopped walking. Were he to go running at Bib and Mr. Hix, they'd both hiss up a fury and then probable point him packing back toward home. That was what his brain was warning.

Inching through the heavy scrub, Yoolee couldn't yet see either Hacksaw Hix or his uncle, but the old gent was yelling. His voice pitched higher than Uncle Bib's, and he seemed plenty excited. Yoolee couldn't make out any exact words on account both Kicker and Cain were barking their heads off. They were usual quiet animals, Yoolee recalled, contained and in their owner's control. Not right now.

Stumbling through the brush, Yoolee felt the ground becoming mucky and wet. Mud splashed up with almost every step.

He came to a slough.

The pond water looked dark and dangerous deep to swim across. Yoolee wasn't a good swimmer. Add to that the extra heft of the twenty-gauge, so he was of no mind to attempt it. Or even wade. He'd be no more than a fool to chance meeting a gator or a snapper turtle.

More noise was carrying across the water. Now he heard the distant barking of the dogs, and men shouting. And another sound. It was a deep, grunting noise. Snarly, plus a sharp chomp-chomp-chomp of strong jaws, bringing to mind what Bib had said about a boarhog's fangs.

"There's an upper pair of curly tusks that'll sometimes go as long as nine inches. But these ain't the danger, because his canine tusks merely hone a pair of lower rippers. The rips are dangerous little daggers that can puncture a hole through the skull of a dog. Or a man. Add to that five hundred pounds of strength and speed, with a thick plate of pig hide that's near to iron-tough. What ya got, Yoolee, is deadly weapons on a ornery ogre."

Again and again, Yoolee heard the chomp-chomp of powerful jaws; added to that a very strong and sickening odor. And it called to mind more things that his uncle had told him.

"When a hunter hears a chomp sound," Uncle Bib had added, "it means the boar is using his tusks to sharpen his rippers."

Bib had also remarked that no growed-up boar could honest be called stupid. "The animal is whip smart," he said. "In fact, he can outthink most men. In a fight, a hog knows how to position himself down-wind of his enemy. His nose can tell him where the hunters and dogs are located yet not reveal his own location."

Yoolee Tharp had a lot to think about as he squinted into the late-afternoon sun, wondering how to figure his way around the slough and remain alive.

"Uncle Bib!" he wanted to holler. Yet he somehow managed to hold quiet and allow his brain to work instead of his mouth.

Just by chance, Yoolee happened to glance upward and saw several buzzards overhead, slowly drawing their black circles in the sky. Why were they circling? It took Yoolee Tharp only an instant to know.

Somebody, or something, was about to die.

Buzzards always knew.

It took a spell, but he final spotted the men and their dogs across the water. At such a distance even Bib appeared tiny, and Mr. Hix was a speck. Because of the thick brush and ferns, he could see the pair of hunters only from the belt up, and little of Kicker and Cain. Once in a while he spotted the nervous lashing of a high tail. All four moved slowly to his right. Glancing left, he almost stopped breathing when he saw a brawny body, all black, yet starting to gray with age. Because of the dense palmetto he couldn't see a head, but the tail was crowbar straight. It was tufted, as Bib early said, at its tip.

Watching, Yoolee's throat seemed to want to choke.

For a moment, the entire animal remained out of sight. Then, stalking very slowly, he moved into full view, looking like an ox with shorter legs. A large and hairy head. Its snout was pointed direct at where the hunters and dogs had been. The boar moved in the same direction, appearing in no hurry, not making any ugly chomping noise with its jaws.

A quick check of the upper lace of the cypress trees told Yoolee that a slight breeze was blowing from right to left—away from the hunters and toward the boar. Such a wind put the boarhog safe and the other four in harm's way.

At times the wind shifted, blowing almost directly into Yoolee's face, so he could inhale the animal's scent: strong, mean, and bitter.

The hog's stink made Yoolee gag.

To his right, Kicker and Cain were no longer barking. The dogs trotted around in circles, mostly out of sight, probable with their noses near the ground to taste any hint of the animal.

"He's back yonder!" Yoolee yelled, helplessly realizing at once that the constant noise of swamp frogs had swallowed up his words. His heart felt as though it was pounding up inside his head.

Yoolee sudden saw how fooly it was, seeing as he was too far away to be any help or even be heard.

Why, he was wondering, were Mr. Hix and Uncle Bib working away from the boarhog instead of toward it? Didn't make a lick of sense. They ought to turn around pronto to meet the thing and shoot it. Kill him proper, so he wouldn't keep on goring folks.

"Turn around!" he tried again. "Turn!"

As he moved along the water's edge, all his yelling was useless. He was too distant. The breeze was blowing into his face sometimes, bringing back all of his futile warnings. It was like shouting to his own self. Or to an uncaring swamp.

The hunters kept moving to Yoolee's right, across the expanse of deep water. The dogs went the same way. That smart old boar had backtracked, circling around behind all of them. For sure that hairy hunk knew where they were and whichaway headed. The confused men kept darting one way, then another, splashing their boots through heavy mud and doing little more except to wear out. Kicker and Cain appeared to be acting likewise.

Not the boar. The animal was strolling on solid turf, biding his time as if planning to attack where and whenever it suited him. Yoolee even saw the animal flop down for a rest.

There wasn't anything Yoolee could do to warn Bib or Mr. Hix, and the hopelessness was beating him like a drum.

He tried screaming at the two men again, to no

avail. But he still kept it up until his throat turned hoarse, as though he was hollering fog. Yoolee felt like crying. He knew what Uncle Bib and Mr. Hacksaw Hix and their dogs didn't know. No doubt all four thought they were hunting pig meat, yet they were dead wrong.

The brute was stalking them.

▲ Chapter 16 ▲

Yoolee had to act. But how?

In desperation, a plan formed in his mind. Sloshing through the shallow water, he spotted two fallen logs. Twins, lying side by side on a mud bank as if waiting for him.

A nearby cypress, standing tall in the black muck, was being choked by a strangler fig and several other thick vines that gripped its massive trunk. All he needed was a few lengths of vines to rope the two fallen logs together.

It wasn't easy to do.

First off, he hadn't thought to bring along a knife. This meant the vines couldn't be too stout to break by biting or bending them back and forth, yet they had to be thick enough for lashings.

Yoolee began by floating the logs beside one another, twisting a vine to snug them together tighter than two fingers. Working in the shallow water proved to be a muddy business. The hardest part was knotting the ends of the vines firmly enough to hold. A pesky swarm of gnats didn't help. They forced Yoolee to duck beneath the surface to escape their making a meal of his head. He paused to smear black muck on his face for protection.

The second vine seemed easier. By fixing the first, he'd seen how to twist the loops into a solid knot.

At last his double-tree raft was completed.

The twin logs proved more than massive enough to support his weight. One log would have done so. But it might roll and dump him off into a wet death. Two logs would float steadier.

Resting a bare foot on each of the trunks, Yoolee started to ease across the dark mirror of water, using the shotgun's butt as a paddle. The pickerelweeds slowed him. Yet he kept on working his twenty-gauge oar, wondering why he hadn't thought to waste a shell. Firing the gun once into the air would have certain got Mr. Hix and Uncle Bib's attention and might have spooked off the boar. Trouble was, Yoolee realized as he paddled, he really didn't have any spare shells to gamble away.

"I might need all three."

Once, over the deeper water, his right foot slipped on the log's moss. It close to made him drop the twenty-gauge into the drink. Had that actual happened, the shotgun would have been gone for keepers.

"Steady," he told himself. "Yoolee Tharp, you mustn't do stupid out here. If'n you lose Velmer's gun, he'll about rake you raw with his belt once Uncle Bib leaves."

He paddled careful, keeping a tight grip on the twenty, wishing he'd had the sense to tie a skinny lanyard of vine through the trigger loop and around one ankle or a wrist. That way, in case the gun went swimming, at least he could fish it dry again.

"I don't cogitate enough. Mama says such to me, and it's truth. At times, I just go charging off and into trouble, like I can't wait to mess myself up. I gotta think. Then do."

To his left, something seemed to be swimming beneath the brown surface, making ripples. A few bubbles appeared. Either a gator, Yoolee decided, or one heck of a big gar. He swallowed. Fighting the urge to paddle faster, he allowed the logs to slow and merely drift. Crouching low, he held his breath, squinting ahead to the hummock of solid land on the opposite shore. No sign of hunters, dogs, or the black boar.

This worried him.

"I don't like it when I can't see that ol' hog. It's safer when I know where he is."

A troubling thought: He was probable moving toward that animal. No doubt the boar knew more than he did. Intently listening, he imagined he heard a single *chomp*. What was it his uncle had learned him about a boar's mouth?

"Awesome jaws, Yoolee," Bib had told him. "A

boar's jawbones contain forty-four teeth." His uncle had held up a warning finger. "And remember, that includes wisdom teeth. A boar's a wise beast. Bigger they be, the wiser. Size means the animal's learned to survive, how to hunt, and also how to kill powerful prey."

Again Yoolee swallowed his fear.

Here he was, floating above a gator on a couple of slippery logs with a gun he'd stolen off Velmer and fixing to paddle toward a big killer hog. Well, first thing, best he push his raft forward and to land. For sure, he couldn't stay floating on deep slough.

He paddled gently, never lifting the shotgun's butt out of the water or splashing it back in again. Perhaps this had attracted the gator.

At first, the far shore didn't seem to be getting any closer. It stayed a distant green. Yet, paddling hard, Yoolee finally began to make headway. Slow and steady. No call to let either the boar or a gator know of his whereabouts. Slow. Steady. Inching forward. Stroke after stroke, he plowed the water behind him.

The butt of his raft nosed to the shoreline, bumping solid ground. It pitched Yoolee forward, forcing his knees to the mossy logs, lowering his body, letting him look ahead through the ferns and palmetto before trying to jump ashore. Getting off wasn't easy. Every time he tried to step forward, the raft beneath his feet snaked backward over the pond again.

The bank was muddy green with slime.

Very nearby, Yoolee saw a rounded pit, as though a huge boulder had dropped and then was picked up and toted off. Curious as to what it was, Yoolee stared at it, then touched it. The muddy earth felt slightly hairy, prickerish. It took a while for him to reason how come. The leftover hair had bristled from the back and flanks of a large hog; it was stiff and mean-feeling like anger.

Standing over the pit, he whispered, "That got dented by a precious big animal." The awesome size made his body shudder.

Listening, he could hear nothing except a few frogs. No sounds from the hunters, dogs, or hog grunts. Even birds had quieted, as though they'd turned too feared to chatter and disrupt the eerie silence. Behind him in the slough pond a bass jumped after a dragonfly, making a sudden splash. Then the swamp was again still.

Glancing down, Yoolee saw the two-toed hoof-prints this monster had punctured into the soft black soil. They were deep holes, partly filled by muddy water. Their depth told him how heavy the animal had to be. He was guessing maybe three times the weight of a growed man.

Paddling across the slough had eaten up time, precious much of it, yet Yoolee knew which direction to travel. Off to the right. All he had to do was head into the wind and follow the boar's deep tracks. The problem was that the critter was now between him and the hunters. Perhaps, instead of tailing the tracks, he ought to strike out wide, attempting to circle around to meet up with Bib and Hacksaw.

"No."

He was afraid to leave the tracks. By following them, he'd at least know the beast was ahead of him.

Something made him stop. A noise. It was a soft, woody *coo* sound that might have been made by a dove. But this whistle didn't come from a bird. Nor was it far away.

The warning had come from behind his back, and then, a breath later, he once more heard the bird sound.

Cooooo.

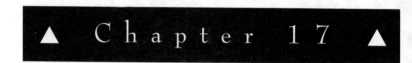

▲ Chapter 17 ▲

▲ ▲ ▲

Again Yoolee Tharp saw the face.

But this time the Calusa stayed in sight instead of dissolving into the ferns and saw grass.

Clouded eyes stared at him, unblinking and unafraid. The bronze face seemed to have been cast out of metal, incapable of movement. The Calusa intended to be seen.

Yoolee gasped.

For years he'd heard some folks warn of how warlike the Calusa were—or had been a long time ago. Others, younger grownups, insisted that the Calusas had disappeared. The few that remained, they said, were shy, rarely seen, but spoke a few words of English.

Now, confronting this aging face, Yoolee oddly felt little fear. Only a warming rush of adventure, as though the two of them respected each other as hunters.

A twig of greenery was slowly pushed aside and Yoolee noticed a bare tawny chest. Havilah had been wrong. This person wasn't a woman but a man.

The gray head offered a slight nod, a greeting without words, and continued its welcoming stare. Something in the man's manner made Yoolee believe that the Calusa, should he desire, could slip out of sight in less than a blink, vanishing without as much as the brush of a twig or the crackle of a dry, trodden leaf.

Yoolee waited, wondering if he himself ought to make the next move and advance toward the man. Meanwhile, the Calusa offered no more than a nod. Then, very slowly, he lifted his right arm; there was no fist, and the fingers stretched open to a star, as if to show he held no weapon.

Yoolee did likewise.

Only then did the Calusa smile. But it certain wasn't what anyone would call a broad ear-to-ear grin. As Yoolee started forward, so did the Calusa. Both of them stepped slowly, with caution, until they were almost near enough to touch. No handshake took place.

"My name's Yoolee Tharp."

Taking another step closer, the stranger stretched out a hand to touch the boy's hair. Yoolee stood still, barely breathing. Eventually the man retracted his hand and smiled, not using his mouth but his black eyes, in each a tiny white-star glimmer.

He pointed to Yoolee's cornsilky head.

"Pretty," he said. "Hair that sings."

Yoolee realized that his own face was looking confused, so the Calusa said more.

He pointed a fingertip to his own chest. "Henry. Henry Old Panther. You are Hair That Sings." He touched Yoolee's shoulder. "Where is Little Singing Hair?" As he asked, a hand with crooked fingers indicated the height of a shorter child. And both of their new names made Yoolee want to smile.

"Havilah's at home with our mother." He started to point but wasn't at all sure about the direction.

"Come."

Too exhausted to argue, Yoolee accepted the Calusa's single word of help, convinced that he should follow. Henry Old Panther seemed to savvy all that was happening and why Yoolee had been trailing after the two noisy men and their barking dogs. Perhaps he also knew the reason for the shotgun and appeared not to fear it.

Walking behind Henry Old Panther, the boy observed long white hair, a shirt of rainbow colors, a grass rope that supported short deerhide trousers. No shoes. His left leg looked lean but healthy; the right, however, had been badly crippled. The Calusa limped. He carried two weapons: a lance as long as his height and, on his hip, a knife in a sheath that seemed so much a part of him that it appeared to sprout from a hipbone. The lance seemed to be a natural extension of the old calusa's arm.

When the barrel of the twenty-gauge whacked against a mangrove trunk, creating a sharp noise, the Calusa turned to shake his head.

The gesture made Yoolee feel aware that perhaps silence was wiser than noise.

After a while and a great many steps, Yoolee suspected they were walking an arc of a large circle. Earlier he'd been breathing foreign odors he couldn't identify, but now the flavors of home seemed to be returning: swamp cabbage, muscadine, and wild coffee.

Ahead, the stranger never stopped, not even a one time, to look around or check on his direction. But at last he rested to fill his lungs with air, then turned and pointed through a gap between a pair of tall fan palms.

Yoolee squinted. In the distance, he recognized the distinct crown of the giant banyan tree that stood a short trot north of where Uncle Bib usual parked the Ford.

Henry Old Panther nodded. "You go." He held up four fingers. "Men and dogs come before sun falls. All tired. No food. The animal they hunt killed a fawn and now sleeps. So will Henry." He pointed at the trail from the Ford to the shack. "Go now, Hair That Sings. Go to Little Singing Hair." He paused. "You fear the loud one? Man smells sick and beats with belt?"

"How do you know all this?"

Saying nothing, the Calusa used his bent fingers to touch his own ears and eyes. He placed his hand over his mouth and then pointed to his brain.

Yoolee understood.

"I watch." Henry Old Panther paused. "How strange to speak. My children's children teach English talk to me. Long time, I talk to Henry and moon. No else. Soon I go away. Far."

"Where?"

"Nine Man Tree." He looked at Yoolee. "Not yet. I go when Spirit Mother calls."

With a polite nod, he limped out of sight, disappearing into a jungle of low-growing palmetto. All was silent. On the ground there was no sign of footprints, no toe marks, as if Henry Old Panther was merely a fog to float by, leaving all of Florida untouched. The Calusa had melted away as silently as smoke.

Slowly the boy walked down the trail, heading for home. Yet he no longer feared being alone. Instead, he felt taller, stronger, and the shotgun an ounce lighter. Now he was more than just Yoolee Tharp.

He'd also become Hair That Sings.

▲ Chapter 18 ▲

▲ ▲ ▲

Upon reaching Uncle Bib's motorcar, Yoolee was amazed that someone else had also arrived there, a lady holding a makeup kit.

Mimosa May Sugarman jingled a ring of keys.

"Don't try to stop me," she warned Yoolee. "See these? Bib forgot 'em. Took me a while, but I final located them hanging on a nail in your place." She tried to unlock the driver's door. "And I sort of know how to drive because that scalawag uncle of yours learnt me."

"Miss Sugar," Yoolee asked the lady in surprise, "are you really fixing to leave without Bib?"

She smirked. "About as fast as anybody left anywheres. All you people will see is my dust. I'm so dreadful sick of this one and only dress that I could burn and bury it." She scowled. "Doggone door is rusted shut. And I'd bet this Ford is itching to hightail out of this bug hole worse'n I cotton to."

She gave the door a kick. Miss Sugar seemed

shocked when it opened, because her mouth opened too.

"If you leave, how'll Bib git home?"

"That scamp who left us all to go pig-hunting, can walk, fly, crawl, wade through water or straddle a barrel and pretend it's a mule. I never want to see that... that...I can't think up a word sorry enough to suit him. Leaving me here to go rambling off with that Seesaw person."

"Hacksaw."

"Whoever he is, Mr. Bible Alderkirk is welcome to my share." Sugar was laughing. "Oh, I wish I could see the tribulation on Bib's face when he knows his Ford's gone on without him."

Yoolee just stared. This lady couldn't possible know about the monster he'd seen out yonder, its size, or all the killing it could do. Miss Sugar never knew a boy named Walton Baggitt or a little tyke of a gal, Lottie Maddux. She hadn't seen the remains of a giant man, Mr. Trace Jessup. But it wasn't Sugar's blame. A city woman didn't study on boarhogs.

Heaving herself into the driver's seat, Miss Sugar, who wasn't exactly what anyone might call skinny, managed to mash the horn button.

Wooga. Woooooo-ga.

Not to be outblared, she honked out another blast of cussing. "Dang this key ring. There's gotta be a dozen keys here, and I'd bet that Bib hisself don't know what locks half of 'em fit."

The Ford wouldn't start.

"Spark? Gas? Choke?" Miss Sugar was pounding the wheel with a fist. "I'd enjoy giving a choke to Bib Alderkirk. Oh, wouldn't I ever. And if I never see that no-count again, it'll be too blessed soon." Pound. Pound. "Why don't this she-devil start?"

"I know why. Uncle Bib sometimes has the same problem. But maybe you'd best wait patient until he returns, because he'll want to…"

"Skip the advice," Miss Sugar snapped. "Why won't it kick in?"

"You flooded it. That's what Bib says, but don't ask me whatever it means, 'cuz us Tharps don't own a Ford or anything. So I reckon a car floods like a boat and then sinks."

Wooga.

Miss Sugar blew the horn again, this time on purpose, because her temper seemed to need water in its radiator. The Ford, however, stayed totally cold.

"Maybe," Yoolee suggested, "you ought to raise up the hood place. That's usual what Uncle Bib does when it won't. The hood's up front."

"I know where a hood is! But I'm not sticking my face anywhere near an engine. Those things can blow up."

"Could be you're out of gas."

Sugar studied the dashboard, her eyes darting

from one gadget to another until she tapped one of them with a painted red fingernail.

"Fuel," she said. "It's on E. Empty!"

"Well, you might be wrong about that, Miss Sugar. Honest. Bib took us riding a couple of times. He claims that unless the engine's running, nothing on the dashboard tells anything. Bib says..."

"I don't care what that rascal says. Or what you say. Please let me escape from this swamp or wherever we are. Please."

Sugar started to sob.

Yoolee patted her shoulder. "Steady now, Miss Sugar. Take it easy. Just you tarry, because Uncle Bib'll be coming back right soon."

A pair of red eyes, rimmed by some wet black stuff that was smearing on her face, stared back at him. "How would you know?"

"Henry said so."

"Henry? You said he was Hacksaw."

"That's somebody else. I meant Henry Old Panther."

Miss Sugar looked very confused and was working up another cry. "I want to go back home." She busted into tears. "What I really want is a bubble bath. Oh, just to be clean again and sleep in my own private bed. And not smell a goat."

Dogs barked.

Turning around, Yoolee saw Bib, Mr. Hix, Kicker,

and Cain heading their way. Both men seemed close to falling down exhausted. With the Winchester over his shoulder, aimed forward, and his fingers gripping the blue of the barrel, Bib was trudging as if he weren't able to slap at a chigger. Mr. Hix could barely move. The men were muddy-legged to way above both knees. Neither dog looked much healthier. One favored a sore paw.

Bib walked up to the open car window and peered in at his lady friend, who was seated behind the steering wheel. "Going somewheres, honey bun?"

"Out of here, that's certain. How could you forsake me in that shack with those pesky hound dogs that'd growl or snap at me anytime I poke my head out the door? And howl all night. I want to go home, Bib. Right pronto. Hear?"

Resting a tired boot on the edge of the running board, Bib leaned against the car's black metal and sighed.

"Sugar," he said, "you have my apology. And I hope to leave soon as we accomplish what takes doing. That big tusker has slaughtered people, darlin'. Including children." He glanced at Yoolee. "Don't guess my conscience would allow me to leave Ruth Ann and her pair, until…"

"Until I go batty." Crossing her arms, Miss Sugar took a deep breath and let out a long, weary sigh. After a moment or two, she looked at Yoolee and unexpectedly forced a feeble smile. Then she gently touched Bib's hand. "Oh, all right, Bib. We'll see it through to a finish. I can't ask you to desert your family."

Kicker and Cain caused everyone to jump when they suddenly set to barking, noses pointed down trail toward the Tharps' place. Ridges of hair bristled along their spines. Mr. Hix commanded them to hush, and the animals obeyed. Yet they kept glowering and growling as though they disliked whatever they'd heard or smelled.

Bib looked at what ired the dogs. "Velmer?"

Sure enough, Yoolee recognized his pa slowly hobbling up the hill, shouting and waving his skinny arms. His face winced with every step. The dogs started yapping again, lips curled, snarling as though Velmer Tharp was poison. Had not Mr. Hix controlled them, Kicker and Cain would surely have ripped him to ruin.

Velmer stopped.

"Hold off them cur hounds," he whined.

"They're held," Mr. Hix answered. "But if'n I'd be you, Velmer Tharp, I'd not venture too neighborly unless your bowels don't like remaining in one length."

"Make 'em stay put, Hacksaw."

"They be put. It's you that's all ruckus."

Velmer stood still. "Somebody stole my gun. My twenty."

"I took it," Yoolee said. "Because I wanted to go hunting with Uncle Bib and Mr. Hix. Nobody stole it. I just borrowed it."

Velmer cussed. "You probable busted it or fouled up the action." His hand went to his belt buckle. "I oughta whup ya, boy. Whup ya till ya can't stand."

"You do," Bib told him, "and you'll get hung upside down naked and left for the land crabs."

▲ Chapter 19 ▲

Even though Mr. Hix took his dogs home, the Tharp shack was more than filled to crowded.

After supper, Yoolee and Havilah climbed the ladder to their loft to keep out of temper's way. All four grownups were talking or shouting, and nobody was listening up.

"Yoolee, they's all sour on you," Havilah whispered. "On account you took the shotgun to sneak off in the darksome, and gone so long. It fretted Mama sick. You ought to say a sorry to her and speak it nice."

He knew that Havilah was right. Nobody'd spoke to him except to scold. They all looked at him hard-eyed and kept asking how he'd got so dirty.

"All I was fixing to do was to help hunting that hog," he hissed back at his sister.

"Well, you certain put Mama through it," Hav said. "She hung blame on Uncle Bib for going off, and so did Miss Sugar. Them two took on dreadful. Even Daddy covered up his dirty old ears it turned so loud, and both our hounds whined and wouldn't hush. All because of *you*."

Yoolee said nothing. But he felt better when Havilah brought her little face a mite closer to his.

"How come you're so quiet?" she asked.

"Thinking."

"About what?"

"Well, you certain are someday going to be a mother, the amount you talk. You'll drive your children out the door and your poor ol' husband to a jug. Them and the dogs'll probable escape to a highway, and on purpose run out in front of a log truck. At eight, you're already a champion nagger."

"Is that so?" she huffed. "Maybe I had myself a good reason. That's because I fret almost to crazy you might be eaten up, and I'd be out a brother and never git me another'n."

Yoolee grinned. "Oh, so you'd miss me?"

Havilah's face turned sober. "Fearful bad, Yool."

He poked her. "I ain't dead yet."

Her arms darted around his neck and she was saying, "Please don't die on me, Yoolee. My heart just couldn't abide it."

"I won't, Hav."

She loosened her hold. "Promise?"

Yoolee nodded. "Say," he said, trying to cheer her up, "you were right, Hav, about that haggy face. But it weren't no woman. Turned out to be a Calusa by the name of Henry Old Panther. Not that I was lost, or anything like, but Henry sort of steered me home to the banyan tree and Uncle Bib's car."

Havilah blinked. "Honest?"

"Yup. He toted a spear and a knife and he had long white hair, exact like you said, and walked with a gimpy leg. Guess what name he calls *me* by?"

"For leaving us, it oughta be Empty Head."

"Nope. He called me Hair That Sings. I guess that every young Calusa has black hair. So we look different. He also got a name for *you*."

"Like what?"

"He calls you Little Singing Hair."

After a breath of thought, Hav said, "I kind of like that. Hope you're not telling me a story."

"I ain't lying, Havilah. You and I tomfool each other, but we never fib. So let's not turn serious about lies we never tell."

She made a face. "Henry Old Panther?"

Yoolee nodded. "Got me a hunch this Calusa guy has been watching us Tharps for a spell. Claims he knows about Velmer and his cussed belt. I'd even wager that he knows how come Joonyer Cobb stops by here so frequent."

Havilah cocked her head. "Why does he?"

"Because he's sweet on Mama."

"Is that truth?"

"From all I can tell. Seems to me Joonyer's bashful, especial around lady people. Uncle Bib told me one time he was grateful Joonyer stops by here regular to pay respects."

Havilah let out a long breath.

"Well," she said, "I'll be hornswoggled. That's the word Miss Sugar uses when she gits up in the morning only to learn that Bib's gone off hunting with Mr. Hix." Hav giggled. "She used that'n and a passel of other words with a lot more pepper."

Yoolee grinned. "Like which words?"

Hav tilted up her nose. "Them's for me to keep and you to wonder. You think you know so much, Yoolee Tharp. Well, I heard some fancy words you'll never understand." She made a face. "Actual, I'm not certain I savvy even a one, but they sure sounded sinful."

"Tell me just one, Hav."

"Say please."

"Okay...please. Now do it. But don't holler it out loud, because the grownups down below will certain to hear it. And I'm in enough misery for one night. I was lucky Mama fed me." He poked his sister. "Go ahead, say Miss Sugar's wicked word."

"All right. But first you'll have to close your eyes. I don't cotton to have anybody watch me say it."

"Hav, you're worse'n Bib. You both string people along, as Mama says, until everybody's about fixing a fit."

Havilah lifted her chin. "No need to snoot uppity.

Maybe I won't tell you at all."

Yoolee sighed. "Right by me."

"I best whisper it in your ear." Leaning closer, his sister cupped hands around her mouth. "Now promise you won't tell."

"For sure I won't tell whatever I ain't never going to know, because by the time you git around to telling me the word, I'll be too olden and too deaf to hear as much as a gunshot."

"Well, all right. Here goes." Havilah stopped short. "Your eyes are open."

He closed them to a squint.

For almost half a breath, all was quiet. Even the four grownups had for some reason halted their arguing with one another. At that moment, Yoolee Tharp heard something he surely didn't plan on hearing. It had nothing to do with any of Miss Sugar's salty-dog language.

It was a low snort, deep and darksome, as though belched from the bowels of the earth. One vicious grunt that was intended to warn the world of some threatening wrong. A single sound that wanted to cut into anything in its path. The noise seemed to hang in the air like an odor, strong and sharp.

Yoolee's ears tasted pain.

And then Velmer let out a scream of terror that knifed into the night, a cry that almost drew blood. He began to sob like a person about to lose all reason.

Havilah rolled over as close to Yoolee as she could squeeze, her entire body trembling. She felt hotter than fever.

Below the loft Velmer kept up his screaming. "It's come. I swear to God, that thang is come here to kill me!"

▲ Chapter 20 ▲

Uncle Bib cocked his Winchester.

"Vel," he said, "make sure there's slug in your twenty. Birdshot dust won't cut it." Bib raised his voice. "Dang ya, Velmer. Quit standing knock-kneed in your underwear with your mouth slack-jawed. Help me, man."

When Bib opened the door a crack to peek outside, Miss Sugar cranked up her screeching another notch until Ruth Ann slapped her quiet. Sinking to the floor, Sugar curled up to hold a knee with one hand. The other covered her face.

"Forgive me," Ruth Ann said as she crouched close to Bib's lady. "Please forgive me, Sugar."

From under the shack both Possy and Ladylove set to barking. Right after the goat bleated in terror, there was a gurgling that slashed the goat's complaint to silence.

"That ol' boar's turned mad in the head," Bib said over his shoulder. "Can't see him, but I think he just killed the goat out of pure ornery." To Ruth Ann he added, "I've heard more'n once they'll do such. Go on a killing spree worse'n a wolf among sheep, and slaughter everything they see." He stepped outside for a quick look and came back in. "Lord, I saw him. Never seen a boarhog near the size of a cow! He's five hundred pound."

Havilah struggled to free herself of Yoolee's arms. "I gotta see."

Creeping halfway up the loft ladder, Ruth Ann said, "Hold tight to your sister, Yoolee. Don't let 'er loose, hear?"

"Yes'm."

Stepping off the bottom rung, Ruth Ann went to the corner where Sugar lay to put her arms around the quivering woman. "There now, Sugar. Rest easy. Everything'll be all right."

Underneath the shack, both Tharp dogs were growling like bears. Yoolee couldn't believe it, but it sounded as if they were attacking the boar. One yelped. Then Yoolee heard a sharp *crack*. The animal must have charged and smashed one of the weaker shack stilts. The entire structure tilted. A corner began to sag.

"Bible," said Ruth Ann, "You and Velmer's got to go outside and kill that thing before it…"

A second crack, much louder than the first, prompted the entire shack to keel. Crockery fell and smashed. Pots slid off the stove. The table and two benches went skidding along the steeply slanted floor

147

and ruptured a thin wall.

"He ain't after them dogs," Velmer said in a voice like an omen. "That devil's after *us*. He'll get us until we's all dead. Then eat us."

There were more cracking sounds. Yoolee's world turned upside down as the damaged shack splintered, then crashed to the ground. Their bed-tick, stuffed with straw, was over his head and Havilah's. His sister's naked foot was wiggling under his chin as she struggled.

Somebody fired a gun. Velmer's twenty?

"Damn it, Vel. What ya shootin' at?"

As dirt and dust clouded his eyesight, Yoolee felt his mother's touch and heard her voice. "Don't budge. You kids stay right calm and don't be sticking up your heads, hear?" She recovered them with their sleeping tick.

"I'm bleeding," Yoolee heard his pa say. "Now that boarhog'll smell me certain. He's come to git a purchase on me with them awful rippers." Velmer's voice became high-pitched. "I know. Because I seen that Satan up close. Tore at me, he done. He torn my insides."

Another dog howled his pain.

Wham!

"Doggone," said Bib, "I missed him."

"Hell ya did," Velmer said. "I just got fresh pig blood splattered in my eyes. You nicked a piece of that heller."

"Yool?" a tiny voice asked.

Feeling Havilah's hand on his hair, Yoolee told her, "I'm right here. Don't worry, Hav. I'll mind you. I won't scat off again and leave you lonesome."

"I peeked out and saw it, Yoolee," his sister whispered. "It near to run right over me. Oh, Yool, it's bigger'n a manatee. I'm so feared that I threwed up."

Yoolee hugged her. "I'm afraid too." This was no story. His bowels felt as though they'd bust out loose at any moment, and whatever it was deep inside his belly, it certain was fluttering. And to think he'd pulled his pa's scattergun off the wall to hunt this curse of a critter like it be a squirrel. The thought made him shudder.

"I dropped my shell," Velmer wailed.

"Find it," Bib told him. "I can hear that critter battling the dogs. He can bust through these rotted planks anytime he's of a mind. Keep the gun aimed at his sound, Vel, but don't fire. Let's not waste ammo until he charges."

"Yoolee, is the boar going to destroy Possy and Ladylove?" Havilah asked. "I don't want 'em to die, Yool. Don't let 'em."

"I won't."

The boy wondered how he could allow himself to speak out such fooly promises to his sister. Right now, the hounds weren't a worry. It was his baby sister.

Little Singing Hair. He'd not cotton to wake up to another morning sun without Havilah's nearness and dearness. Mama and Uncle Bib weren't eight. They could, he prayed, look after theirselves.

Another earsplitter of a noise caused Yoolee to glance to the right, just as a flimsy wall got battered into no more than shards of shack wood.

Nearby, a grayish and hairy snout appeared, its tusks reddened shiny with fresh blood, mouth foaming in frenzy. Clenched in the great jaws was what seemed to be the tattered spine of a dog. It quit panting just long enough for its teeth to crunch the bone to fragments.

Specks of blood misted the moonlight.

As a deep snarl rumbled from its throat, its eyes searched for another victim. Charging forward, the forked hoofs trampled into the household debris, intent on a fresher target.

"God!"

Yoolee could hear Velmer Tharp's final terrified word.

Twisting around, clinging to Havilah as much in fright as with duty, Yoolee watched in horror as the critter tore Velmer's body. A snap of spine and gushes of body fluids, mostly crimson, exploded all over. Unable to look, Yoolee covered his eyes. Havilah wiggled away. Then, a breath later, he again looked. A giant head whipped around, tusks and jaws closed, gripping a long leathery snake of hide. The animal spat out a belt that was now as lifeless as its owner, and buried his snout into Velmer Tharp's chest.

A woman screamed.

"Oh, Lordy," Yoolee heard Uncle Bib cry, "it's after Sugar! No. No!"

Without aiming, Bib fired again, and the boarhog roared his pain. The noise made Yoolee reach for his sister, but she wasn't within reach. He thought he heard his mother crying. Another agonized dog yelped; its sound was cut short, replaced by the *chomp-chomp* of sharper fangs powered by more forceful jaws. Yoolee's eyes were closed, as his mind plunged into some mysterious madness. Death pounded and pounded its dreadful drum.

His only prayer was a name.

"Havilah?"

Again and again he repeated his simple hope, receiving no answer. Into the dusty darkness he cried a silent scream of terror that he himself was unable to hear.

The nightmare went on and on as though it would never end. Deep grunts seemed to be coming from all sides, plus a sorry sound of powerful jaws crushing both flesh and bone.

After a long while, the noises softened and became less frequent. Then faded away.

The boarhog was swallowed by dark silence.

▲ Chapter 21 ▲

The night thickened.

Above, there was no longer a roof to repel a misty rain. Below, in the wreckage of the shack, no one stirred.

Yoolee cautiously blinked, lying motionless and wondering if his bones had all been busted. He was hurting all over, a pain of some intense, unfillable hunger that ached with every heartbeat. Through the blur he identified his mother as she lay open-mouthed, staring at a mangled body that had been her husband. Uncle Bib lay exhausted. Yoolee could also see Miss Sugar, who still seemed frozen in fear.

Havilah?

Yoolee dared not speak her name aloud, too worried that she couldn't answer. Had the demon carried Little Singing Hair off?

The fingers of Yoolee's right hand began to crawl, as would a dazed spider, twitching at first, then expanding to explore tiny areas of grit and splinters. Then his other hand searched. There was no Havilah to find. If in truth he no longer had a sister, was there any purpose in trying to sit up?

"Havilah?"

"Yool? I be here, Yoolee."

Hearing Havilah's voice was more welcome than a dawn. To him it was a golden sunup of sound.

"Where?" he asked.

"Miss Sugar's got me. We's all soaking wet. When that awful animal come at us, she holded me close and took his meanness."

Yoolee crawled toward the voice.

Havilah had been telling him was true. Mimosa May Sugarman, with her ample arms cradling a little blond girl, looked rubbed raw. Her clothes were torn, and several welts cut into her flesh. Snug inside this comforting nest of safety lay Havilah. With a dirty face, she gazed up at him, smiling.

All Yoolee could do was draw closer in order to kiss Miss Sugar on a chubby cheek that was now missing all traces of what she called her cosmetics. And Bib called her war paint. Although now plain and pale, for the first time Sugar looked to be a truly beautiful lady.

"Yoolee," Hav asked, "are you sound?"

He grinned. "I am now." Closing his eyes in rapture, he inhaled all of a wet little-girl smell.

"Is Uncle Bib alive?" Hav asked her mother.

"Yes," said Ruth Ann, pulling both her children to her to snuggle warm. "Vel's dead, but five of us made it through the night. Be daylight soon. Mockingbirds already up. Listen."

Yoolee heard them, searching their memories for a song to sing. Mockingbirds had no tune of their own. Merely an echo among the high, wet leaves.

Yoolee cautiously ventured outside, not far, to empty his bladder, feeling the relief of a day's first habitual chore. One by each the others shook themselves awake, rubbed eyes, and in damp clothes tended to one another.

Duty demanded to bury the dead.

The battered and bled-dry carcass of Velmer Tharp was slowly lowered, by vines, into the yielding black muck of a Florida morning. Hardly anyone spoke any words as loose dirt hid him forever. Ruth Ann closed her eyes, raised her face to Heaven, and said, "We forgive you, Velmer Tharp. Here below, we all cleanse our souls by washing away all you done. Amen."

As they were smoothing the last handfuls of topsoil over Velmer's grave, Yoolee couldn't help thinking how he'd no longer have a goat and a pair of lazy dogs. He'd miss them. But he'd never miss his father.

Soon after the burial, Deputy Joonyer Cobb arrived by kicker boat. He couldn't believe the mess that once had been a home.

"Mercy," the lawman said, shaking his head at the havoc that lay everywhere. "That ol' critter surely paid you folks company." Taking a step closer to the mound

155

of grassless earth, he added, "Don't guess I have to inquire who's deceased." Removing his cowboy hat in respect, he said, "Can't honest say to y'all that I'm sorry."

"Glad you come, Joonyer," said Bib. "Thanks."

"And do stay." Ruth Ann tried to smile. "I found some grits to boil, along with turnip root, poke salad, and a crookneck squash. We still got pepper sauce to sparkle it all. No jowl or peas. Can't offer you nothing fancier."

"I'll help fix," Sugar said.

"You up to doing?" Ruth Ann asked her, tenderly touching the bruised welts on the woman's shoulder and arms. "You been stomped on awful."

Holding her head higher, Sugar said, "Don't you worry. I'll mend." Then on purpose she made Ruth Ann laugh when she added, "My first date with Bib got rougher than last night."

After that, Yoolee was surprised to see something he'd never before seen. Joonyer Cobb moved to stand close to his mother and then curved a stout arm around her shoulders. The big deputy's beefy hand patted her the gentle way you'd pet a kitten. Without much thinking, Yoolee joined the pair of them, and so did Havilah. All four were sudden standing together like the solid corners of a table.

Bib noticed and cracked an approving grin.

"Like I earlier said," he told the constable, "you're

better'n welcome here, Joonyer Cobb. Do stay, unless duty is pressing you to leave. If so, maybe I ought to tarry around until that animal's ended."

"No need," Joonyer said. "The Tharps got *me* now to watch out for 'em." He glanced at a pleased Ruth Ann. "Permanent if'n they'll have me. Been doing such for years." Joonyer studied his boots. "I never took a trespass at your sister, Bib. Not even a one time. Yet I do got feelings for Ruth Ann, and I'd like to hope she fancies me. So I will gladly head up this family." Joonyer ventured a shy smile. "If I git lucky, maybe we'll all be Cobbs."

"Hope so." Eyeing the smashed-up shelter, Bib asked, "You aim to repair this place and reside?"

Joonyer shook his head. "Nope. I'm fixing to carry 'em away to start fresh." He looked direct at Yoolee. "Providing I can recruit this adventurous youngster to lend a hand and hammer."

"Count me in," Yoolee said.

Havilah chimed in. "Me too."

"But first things first," Joonyer said to Bib. "We best tally up our guns and shells, yours and theirs. On account that creature's still roaming out yonder, possible nearby. You agree?"

"I do," Bib told him.

It turned out they had Uncle Bib's big Winchester rifle. A thorough search produced both of Velmer's scatterguns, but no shells. Not a one. As the two men debated about leaving by car or by boat, an unexpected visitor came. He appeared and stood statue still.

Henry Old Panther.

Surprise dropped Yoolee's jaw and alarmed everyone else.

Nobody spoke. They just stared.

Over his naked shoulder lay a small doe, limp and lifeless. The Calusa allowed the dead deer to slip off, falling to the pine needles with barely a sound. Then he spoke.

"Meat. All eat."

Miss Sugar, with her eyes and mouth wide open, moved to stand directly behind Bib. Her hands were clinging to his hipbones.

Yoolee stepped forward. "Thank you, Henry." As he raised an open right hand, the Calusa copied the greeting. "Mama, this here gentleman is Mr. Henry Old Panther. He calls me Hair That Sings." Pointing to his sister, Yoolee added, "And Havilah is Little Singing Hair."

"Pretty," said Henry.

"There," Hav told their mother, "you see? It wasn't one of my stories. He's real. And I saw him first, didn't I, Yool?"

"Yup. Havilah's right."

"Come," said Ruth Ann when she'd recovered from the shock, "please eat with us, Mr. Panther. And bless you for bringing food. Do come."

Henry Old Panther didn't come. He stood as if carved in stone until Havilah walked to him, bolder than a bull, and by the hand led him into the family. When she released it, the Calusa timidly touched her hair. Then, without a word, he gathered dry wood and made a fire. Before the coals reddened to gray, he skinned and gutted the deer. His fire, however, was so modestly small that the roasting tortured all hungry nostrils.

Locating a black pot from the debris, Ruth Ann and Sugar boiled grits and greens. Henry gave no sign the venison was ready to carve. He merely added tiny twigs to the fire, in no hurry.

Havilah, able to wait no longer for a feast, took a deep inhale of the roast's tempting fragrance, and told Henry, "You best hurry the cookery."

The Calusa remained silent for a time. Then, with barely a twitch of a shy grin, he grunted one quiet word to her, as though sharing a secret.

"Patience."

"Why," Havilah asked him, pointing at the low flames, "is your cooking fire so puny? It ought to be bigger."

"White man build big fire. **Stand back.** Calusa do little fire. Sit close."

▲ Chapter 22 ▲

Bib pulled Yoolee aside.

"Young sir," he confronted him, "Joonyer and I have a few protection duties to take care of. Your job is to keep a watch at Havilah and yourself. Can you handle it?"

"Sure can."

"Neither you nor your sister are to go rambling off, not to look for the boarhog or for that Calusa, who slipped away without a farewell. You're both to stay here in plain sight, like you've been glued or nailed down. Hear?"

"I hear ya, Uncle Bib."

"I'm fretful about your ma." Bib knelt to stare Yoolee in the eye. "Ruthie's took quite a lot of torment in the recent hours, and I don't guess she's able to swallow more misery. Or worry. Do you understand?"

"You bet so."

"You ain't to monkey with a gun, be it yours, mine, or Joonyer Cobb's. Behave, and just maybe I might allow you to drive the Ford."

"Honest?" Yoolee jumped.

Bib punched him easy. "Truly, providing you can manage to forsake mischief." He looked over at Havilah. "It's high possible that your little sister will consider a try at finding Henry Old Panther. Do not let Havilah stray." Bib paused to point up at the sky. "Yoolee, can ya see those black birds up yonder?"

"Buzzards."

"Scavenger birds got a way of smelling what's dead or dying. Don't ask me how. For us down here on the ground," Bib said, as he stomped his boot to the sand, "those buzzards be a warning. Like a snake's rattle. They are alerting us to danger or death."

"Uncle Bib, are you trying to spook me?"

His uncle nodded.

"Indeed so. I want you and Havilah to be as frightened as I am. We all seen, last night, what a boarhog gone mad is capable of. I doubt he's dead, Yoolee." Bib rubbed a brawny arm. "Gives me goose bumps to know he's lurking out yonder, on the prowl for prey. Any animal of his dimension gnaws a lot of chow. That demon is a walking appetite." He mussed Yoolee's hair. "We got to be respectful of this beast. And like I told you days ago, fear is a form of intelligence, to prevent us all from doing foolhardy."

Yoolee swallowed, then twisted around to look all about, just to keep himself on the alert.

"Remember," said Uncle Bib as he walked away,

"you are assigned to be Havilah's watchdog. So watch."

"I promise."

Grabbing his sister's hand, Yoolee led her over to the remains of the shack, now no more than a fallen trash heap.

Sugar was giving Ruth Ann a hand sorting through rained-on trash that had once been a home. After the two women hefted up a cumbersome tabletop with three of its legs busted off, Ruth Ann said, "Sugar, you don't seem the same woman I first met."

"I'm not. Thanks to that awful animal, I've maybe learned what matters." Sugar glanced at Yoolee and Havilah. "Meeting y'all, especially seeing Bib with your youngsters, has made me newborn." She sighed. "In a sense, Ruth Ann, I'm jealous of you. I was married once. But because I'm unable to bear children, my husband left."

"I'm...I'm true sorry, Sugar."

The woman smiled. "Well, I somehow discovered your brother. Mr. Bible Alderkirk is one prince of a man. When he asks me to marry him, and he's been threatening to, I want y'all to know that I'll do him decent. And make him a tidy home." Sugar shook her head as she smiled. "Ruth Ann, the place Bib used to live in looked far worse than your busted-up place."

Both women laughed.

"It's strange," Ruth Ann said, "Velmer's gone, but

my heart feels happier than it has for a number of years. And there's another reason." She rested a hand on Sugar's shoulder. "I've never had myself a sister. Until now. I'm so very grateful that Bib's found *you*."

"Well, I'm pleased as punch," Sugar said, "that you and the children will have the constable around. Only met him once, but he's like Bib. Joonyer's a gentleman."

With one ear, Yoolee had been listening to the grown-up talk, still keeping an eye on Havilah.

He leaned closer to her.

"Hav, if'n we're smart, you and I best not total up losses but thank our good luck. Mama's got Joonyer Cobb, and so do we. Bib's met Miss Sugar. Best of all, we got each other."

"Maybe," said Havilah, "we're nearing rich."

Yoolee pinched her and grinned. "Hey. We're already there."

"And," his sister went on, "we'll be seeing Henry, I bet, whenever we least expect. He'll be visiting us."

Havilah's little-girl faith reached inside Yoolee, causing him to bite his lip, then turn away. He pretended to be looking off into the mist of the swamp, at the tops of very tall cypress trees, searching for the only Calusa he'd ever known.

"When we were all eating deer meat," Hav said, "Henry was here. Then before I could even blink, he was gone."

Yoolee nodded. "Far away," he said softly.

"But he'll be coming back," Havilah insisted.

Yoolee rested a light arm on Little Singing Hair's shoulder. "Henry Old Panther will always be around for people like you and me, who can imagine they see his face. He will be watching over us as long as there's flowers in Florida."

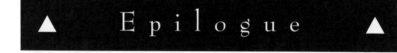

▲ Epilogue ▲

The trail was easily followed.

Because of the Evil One's massive size and weight, the hoofprints cut deep and filled with rainwater.

For many seasons, Henry Old Panther had tracked this animal. Only once had he been eagerly careless, impatient—and his leg paid the price of imprudence. But then the boar was younger and not wounded. Now, Henry could see, the tracks were uneven because the tusker had walked a path of pain. Rain had rinsed the blood away. Soon, however, there might be new blood, fresh and shining, giving off its bittersweet odor.

Would it be Henry's blood or the boar's?

"Yes, old Hell Hog, you and I fight even now. We both limp under the load of life. And death. But I am resolved to outlive you, even if only for one breath."

Burdened by fatigue, Henry Old Panther's body cried for the final sleep, to recline in the darkness of that endless night that promises no dawn. Passing the rough bark of a turkey oak, he inhaled the pleasures of mistletoe, larkspur, and wild rhubarb. Also, he smelled the boar, pondering if the beast he pursued could also smell a Calusa.

Creeping through the trees, Henry whispered a farewell to each and every one: maple, hickory, oak, yew, holly, sweetgum, pine, and here and there, cabbage palmetto. He wanted to say goodbye to the anhinga, to bears, bobcats, possum, mink, gopher turtles. And the nocturnal armadillos with their nine bands of armor. After tonight, he would not visit them. Nor would they remember him.

Ahead, great lungs were laboring with every snorting breath, unable to sustain travel or escape. The boar would never hunt again. But there was no hatred in Henry's heart.

"We who die," he said, "Will greet each other as brothers."

The scent grew stronger.

Beware, the Calusa silently warned the beast, for the odor of Henry Old Panther has also strengthened to alert the mighty snout that a warrior stalks this night with a lance and a knife.

He hadn't informed the nice people who tended the pretty children that their enemy was deeply wounded. The Hell Hog still deserved to be honored. In a way, he had been the prince of all pigs, a baron boar, a stud whose seed in many a seasoned sow planted the burliest of beasts.

A Killer King.

Coming closer in the gloom, Henry squinted to recognize the large one heaving in hurt, unable to rise or run. With caution, the Calusa's grip tightened on the shaft of his lance, raising it to a level position of attack. *The hunter,* he thought, *yet lives within my bowels.*

Stepping slowly, as he'd learned so long ago from a white egret, he advanced to stand at last above the wounded boar. A stinging smell of blood punctured his nose.

His spear cocked.

Now?

No. It would be a coward's blow to bury a lance tip into so injured an animal. Must he prove his manhood against a feeble foe unable to rise? Slowly, lowering the lance, he knelt to perform what he never imagined he would dare do. He touched the boar's flank. It felt hairy and rough, stiff with dried dirt. Warm. Hot. A body fighting to live. Too noble, too proud to be hurried into the silent shadow.

Resting his weapon, Henry said, "Do not be afraid to die, great one. You will not hunt alone in the blue beyond. I shall walk at your side. Two hunters, you and I. Hell Hog and Henry."

Raising his head, the boarhog stared at the old Calusa, then lowered his tusks forever. After a while, the brute's steamy breathing could no longer be heard. For several moments in the swamp, all sound suspended. Even the frogs were still. In the distance, one cricket inspired an entire choir to serenade the night with their anthem. Seated, his backbone resting against a fanpalm's shaggy bark, the worn warrior closed his eyes. One by one, crooked fingers released their grip on the lance.

High in the uppermost twigs and delicate cypress lace of the Nine Man Tree, a wren warbled her sweet song of welcome, and the muddy feet of Henry Old Panther began an effortless climb into the clouds.

Spirit Mother opened her arms.

About ▲ the ▲ Author

Robert Newton Peck's first novel was the highly acclaimed *A Day No Pigs Would Die*. He has written more than sixty books, including the sequel, *A Part of the Sky*, and he is also the winner of the Mark Twain Award for his *Soup* series of children's books. Many of his novels are deeply rooted in rural Vermont, where he grew up.

Rob plays jazz and ragtime piano, and tends eleven mustang horses and two cats. He and his wife, Sam, reside in Florida, the setting for *Nine Man Tree*.

Also by Robert Newton Peck:

A Day No Pigs Would Die
A Part of the Sky
Soup
Soup and Me
Soup for President
Soup's Drum
Soup on Wheels
Soup in the Saddle
Soup's Goat
Soup on Ice
Soup Ahoy
Soup 1776